WIN A DATE WITH TAD HAMILTON!™

WIN A DATE WITH TAD HAMILTON!

BY **CRISTINA FOX**

BASED ON THE MOTION PICTURE WRITTEN BY VICTOR LEVIN

HarperFestival®
A Division of HarperCollinsPublishers

CHAPTER ONE

Stop the car! Stop the car and get out and run to her!

Rosalee Futch was completely enraptured as she stared at the Rialto Theater's movie screen. Two cars were pulled over on the side of a country road, on a cloudless, moonlit night. The two people driving them had been in love once—they were still in love. But they'd been separated, and Rosalee wanted them to get back together.

It was amazing how she could get sucked into a Tad Hamilton movie so intensely.

Tad was playing a handsome young Army lieutenant named Danny. He stepped out of the car and looked back at Betty—his long-lost love—as she got out of her car, too, leaving the door open. The car radio played a romantic Billie Holiday song that Rosalee couldn't quite place.

Tad Hamilton looked good in a military uniform, Rosalee thought. Just like he looked good in anything—no, everything—else.

"Hello, Betty," he said now. His voice was strong, but his eyes betrayed his emotional state. He was in pain—deep, personal pain—over this woman, over this relationship. "Shouldn't you be at the hospital, looking after a certain other soldier?"

The audience at the only theater in Fraziers Bottom, West Virginia, was completely silent, everyone waiting for Betty's reaction. Beside Rosalee, her friend Cathy Feely was staring at the screen with wide eyes.

"I was afraid I wouldn't find you...afraid I'd never see you again," Betty confessed.

"I thought we decided that's the way it has to be," Danny said. "I thought we'd said our last good-bye."

"Yeah, right," Pete Monash scoffed from the seat on the other side of Rosalee.

"Shh!" she whispered. It was just like Pete to ruin the most romantic film scene ever.

"Quiet!" Cathy added.

On the screen, Betty looked at Danny, who was still keeping his distance. "Danny, I won't say I'm sorry. I won't say I was wrong," she said. "I won't say that you're the only man I've ever loved or ever will love. I won't say that my entire life, leading up to this moment, has been nothing but prelude. All I'll say is that this is my favorite song."

There was a long, torturous pause, and then Danny grinned, and extended his hand toward her, inviting her to dance. Then Betty smiled, and the two of them ran toward each other, kissed like crazy, and then fell into the dance of a lifetime.

Rosalee brushed a tear from her cheek as the credits began to roll. Tad Hamilton's name was listed first. At the sight of it, half the people in the audience burst into cheers and applause—Cathy and Rosalee the loudest among them.

Rosalee couldn't believe it, but she liked this Tad Hamilton movie even better than his last one—if that was possible. Of course, Rosalee knew that she was a sucker for romantic movies and tearjerker endings to those movies. That was a given when it came to Tad Hamilton.

"Okay, you're not going to tell me that you two are seriously buying that ending?" Pete asked. He was one of Rosalee's best friends—they'd known each other practically since birth. But that didn't mean he understood why Rosalee and Cathy were so crazy about Tad Hamilton. To him, Tad Hamilton was just another actor.

By this time, Cathy and Rosalee were sobbing uncontrollably along with the rest of the audience.

"Oh, I see. You can relate to it, because that kind of thing happens all the time here in Fraziers Bottom," Pete continued.

Rosalee wiped her tears and glared at him.

Cathy also ignored Pete's comments and turned to Rosalee. "Do you think Tad Hamilton is as good and decent a person in real life as he is on the screen?"

"Absolutely," Rosalee replied. "You can't fake that kind of humanity."

Pete let his head fall back onto the seat, disgusted with the two of them.

"What do you suppose Tad Hamilton is doing right now?" Cathy asked.

Rosalee considered for a moment. "I bet he's in church."

Tad Hamilton morosely crunched a celery stick. Here he was, at Le Petit Four, one of the best restaurants in Los Angeles, eating celery with drops of rice vinegar because he had to look good.

They were sitting outdoors and he didn't want some tabloid reporter calling in a story about how Tad Hamilton was seen eating a giant steak, and what that might mean about him and his future prospects.

He was out of work right now, which meant he couldn't be packing on the pounds. He had to stay in top shape. He had to be ready to take on the role of a lifetime. Even though no one was offering that right now.

He had to be the only actor in Hollywood whose agent and manager had the exact same name—

Richard Levy. His agent worked very hard for him, and he was driven in a way that usually got Tad work. Usually, but not lately.

And his manager, the other Richard Levy? He was obnoxious and pushy, no doubt about it. He never stopped thinking about whether Tad was earning money, because if Tad was, then he was, too. And if Tad wasn't, like now? His manager was getting anxious about it. And so was Tad.

It didn't matter that he'd had a tremendous date the night before, with a gorgeous girl. It didn't matter that he could still get by on his looks and his reputation—could count on them to get any girl he wanted.

"And then she left?" Richard Levy, his agent, asked after Tad stopped telling the story of his latest conquest.

"Just in time for Laker Fourth Quarter Replay," Tad said.

"One night. I want to be you for one night," his manager, Richard Levy, commented wistfully.

"You might not enjoy it as much as you think," Tad said.

"And I want one girl like that. One time in my life," his manager Richard said.

Tad's agent cleared his throat and tapped the table in front of him. "Can we talk about work for a second?"

But his manager wouldn't stop talking about Tad's night. "You realize that, DNA-wise, there's really very little difference between you and me, right? And yet you...live like a pharaoh."

"No, I don't," Tad said. "A pharaoh could get whatever part in whatever movie he wanted." Tad hadn't wanted to admit it to himself, to anyone, but he did feel as if he were in a bit of a slump. He hadn't gotten a good script to look at in months.

"Well, you don't make it easy on us, Tad," his agent commented.

This was the first time Tad had heard this. "What are you talking about?"

Tad's agent pulled a piece of paper out of a folder. It was a somewhat grainy color photo and looked like it had been printed off the Internet. "This is the shot the paparazzi got."

Tad stared at the photograph, a rough image printed from a Web site that was notorious for capturing celebrities at their worst. The picture showed him in his car, behind the wheel of his Porsche 911 Carrera convertible. Was he driving? *I shouldn't have been,* he thought. In the picture, he had a cigarette and a bottle of liquor in one hand, and the other hand on his date from last night.

"Congratulations," his agent said. "You're actually drinking, driving, smoking, leering, and groping at the same time." He cast a critical look at Tad.

"Which is, on the one hand, just about the coolest thing I've ever seen," his manager said, "and I want you to tell me exactly how you did everything, and in what order—"

"Richard!" his agent interrupted.

"But on the other hand, something like this can be a *little* bad for the image."

"'A little bad?'" his agent scoffed. "It couldn't get much worse."

Tad looked at the photo again. Sure, it was bad. But was it that bad? The girl he'd been with was extremely hot. Wasn't that good for his image?

His manager made a *tsk* noise. "Every time you have an episode like this, people clock it, and, the world being the prissy, narrow-minded place that it is, it hurts you," he said.

Tad's agent tapped the photograph with his finger. "You play characters who have heart. This is a person who will have a heart *attack*."

"If you want, we can get you some kind of action movie, maybe," his manager suggested.

"Or a romantic comedy opposite whatever Gilmore Girl is lying around," his agent offered.

"But in terms of quality films..." His manager looked uncomfortable as he shifted in his chair.

Tad had heard enough. How was this all his fault? "I can't believe you're blaming my unemployment on that photograph!" Tad complained. He had a body of work that was very impressive—hadn't he won a few opening weekend battles in his life? Why couldn't anyone remember that. Why didn't anyone think of that, instead of this stupid picture?

His agent cleared his throat. "Okay, first of all, 'unemployment' is a strong word. You are not 'unemployed.' Dockworkers are unemployed. You are simply 'between million-dollar paydays.'"

"As are we, since we live off a percentage of your paydays." His manager bit his lip when Tad glared at him. "But this is not about us."

"I *feel* like an unemployed dockworker," Tad confessed. "I feel aimless. Lost."

"Yes, but unlike him you can cheer yourself up by buying an island or something," his agent pointed out. "Now, believe me, Tad, no one wants to get you into the next gig more than the two of us."

His manager set down his empty glass. "I have shrink bills that would suck the air right out of your lungs."

Richard the agent glared at Richard the manager. "And not just for our own financial reasons," he said pointedly, "but also because we would like to help you avoid the usual period of temporary insanity that strikes when you are between jobs."

"I am not temporarily insane," Tad protested. But as he said that, he noticed a freckle on his arm that seemed suspiciously to have changed in size and shape. "Is this mole raised?" he asked, holding up his arm for them to examine. Maybe he should visit a doctor. "Where's our check?"

"'Okay,' 'no,' and 'on its way.'" His manager

quickly signaled the waiter to bring them the check.

Tad couldn't believe this drought he was going through. Wasn't there anything out there for him? Suddenly he remembered a recent meeting. "What about that part in the Jimmy Ing movie? I'm perfect for that. I met with the guy. I sang for my supper. I complimented him on his friggin' Dutch Partridge Hound."

"Well," his agent said slowly. "He's taking a breath."

"He's what?" Tad asked, not understanding.

"He's taking a breath. He's hemming and he's hawing. He's pausing before deciding," his agent explained. "He's hemming and hawing and pausing and taking a breath."

It all sounded vaguely insulting to Tad. Why couldn't Jimmy Ing see that he was exactly the right actor for the part? Why did he have to *think* about it? "Well, that's very bad. I don't want him breathing," Tad said.

"This is my point. Six months ago, he never would've breathed. He would've staggered up to you, completely unoxygenated, and begged you to take the part." Richard the agent held up the photo. "And this is only going to make him breathe more."

So maybe his agent and manager had a point. Tad could see that his image had taken a bit of a swan dive lately. "Well, what do we do?"

"We figure out a way to asphyxiate him," his

agent said.

"No." His manager shook his head. "We generate a little *positive* p.r."

Richard the agent glared at him. "What are you, an interpreter now?"

"I'm just saying, we need to do something, Tad, to remind Jimmy Ing, and America, that you are the boy next door."

"I *am* the boy next door!" Tad insisted. "I mean, I used to be the boy next door. Until I moved, and I became the boy from down the block and across the alley, where the screwed-up people live," he said glumly.

His agent nodded. "I got you. You're torturing the metaphor, but I got you."

"Yes—we're on the same page," his manager said.

"So how do we make me back into the boy next door?" Tad asked. "I mean, is there a plan you want to share with me?"

His agent nodded, and a wide smile broke out across his face. At the same time, his manager picked up the check and frowned.

"Oh, yeah, there's a plan," his agent said. "Listen to this."

CHAPTER **TWO**

"Pete? Think fast."

Rosalee grabbed a jar of green olives off the grocery shelf and tossed it to Pete, who was walking down the Piggly Wiggly condiment aisle beside her.

"Rosalee. Don't start."

Next she picked up a small relish jar and lobbed it at Pete, just as he was setting the olives back on the shelf. "Think fast."

Pete caught the pickle relish, looking a little more annoyed this time. "Rosalee, this is a dumb game, and by the way? It reveals a real flaw in your personality."

"Think fast!" Rosalee tossed a jar of pearl onions at him.

"I swear to you," Pete said as he let it drop into his cupped hands, as if he were catching a baseball.

"If you throw another one, I'm going to let it land," he threatened.

"No, you won't," Rosalee teased confidently.

"How do you know?" Pete replied.

Rosalee grabbed a mayonnaise jar and tossed it toward him.

Pete looked like he wanted to scream as he grabbed the jar out of midair. "One day. I mean, one day. I will let it land." He frowned at Cathy, who was laughing along with Rosalee. "Don't *encourage* her."

Rosalee opened the door to Pete's office, which also happened to be the employee lounge, as far as Cathy and Rosalee were concerned. They hung out inside Pete's office almost as much as he did.

The walls of Pete's office were cluttered with an assortment of plaques, certificates, and awards he'd won over the past couple of years as the store manager. "Employee of the Month." "Store of the Year." "Store Manager of the Month." If there was an award Pete hadn't won, Rosalee hadn't heard of it. She could just picture the managers at other Piggly Wigglys in the same region, hoping and dreaming that Pete would retire and move on sometime soon. *They must hate him,* she thought. Not that anyone could really hate Pete—he was too nice a guy. He even let her spend her lunch hour surfing the Web on his office computer.

Rosalee, Cathy, and Pete grabbed their lunches from the refrigerator, and Rosalee sat down at

Pete's desk to check her e-mail. She popped open a can of Pringles potato chips and twisted off the top of a bottle of Yoo-Hoo.

Cathy and Pete both sat down behind her, on the beat-up couch, and Cathy leafed through that day's newspaper as Pete read what he called an "industry" magazine—*Modern Grocer.*

"Rosalee, what's your favorite Pringle? Sour cream and onion, or original?" Cathy asked.

Rosalee finished chewing her latest chip. "Depends on how many you're eating," she said.

"Explain," said Cathy.

Rosalee thought about it for a minute before answering. It was a little embarrassing, but she *had* actually thought about this same topic once before. "Well, the sour cream and onion is a very strong taste, and if you're eating a very small amount, say, half a can, then you want that strength. But if you're eating a great deal more than that, you want the original. It's a cleaner flavor."

Cathy nodded. "I see."

Pete shook his head as he leafed through *Modern Grocer* magazine. "Boy, we are pondering some important questions here this afternoon."

"Yeah, uh, what's new in *Modern Grocer* there, Pete?" Cathy teased.

"It's the swimsuit issue," Pete shot back.

Rosalee clicked the mouse and went to her favorite entertainment-news Web sites. She tossed the empty Pringles can toward the trash basket at the edge of Pete's desk. She was off with her toss, as usual—a couple of inches short. But, also as usual, Pete pushed the trash basket over with his foot so that the can dropped right into it.

It was like some weird kind of organized cleaning routine/ballet they had.

Rosalee was reading the latest scandalous divorce news when a pop-up ad floated across the screen. "Whoa," Rosalee said as she saw Tad Hamilton's gorgeous, smiling face floating in front of her. "Oh my God."

"What is it?" Cathy asked.

Rosalee felt like jumping up and down. She didn't even know why she was bothering to restrain herself. This was incredible! "Win a date with Tad Hamilton!" she read, pointing to the banner on the pop-up ad.

"What?" Cathy still didn't get it.

"It's to benefit Save the Children," Rosalee explained as Cathy leaned over to read the ad.

"Oh, that is so like him," Cathy said admiringly.

"Saving children?" Rosalee nodded. "I know." She thought she heard Pete groan and mumble something disapproving as he skimmed the ad, too, but she didn't care. "Should I enter?" she asked Cathy.

"Why not?" Cathy replied.

"Yeah, heaven is just a mouse-click away," Pete said, sounding thoroughly disgusted with the contest already.

Rosalee quickly read the contest rules. "A mouse-click and a hundred buck donation," she said glumly, feeling a little dejected about her chances now.

"We can raise a hundred bucks," Cathy said. "With your permission, Petey."

"I'm sorry?" Pete sounded as if he weren't interested in the slightest. *But that was okay,* Rosalee thought. She and Cathy could convince him to help them come up with the money. The fact that she'd seen this little pop-up ad just now was a sign, she decided. She was meant to win. Or at least she was meant to donate a hundred dollars to a good cause.

An hour later, she and Cathy were back at work, ringing up customers. Beside each register were the usual spare-penny dishes and the Easter Seals donation jar. But now, thanks to Cathy, each register also had a jar that said: "Help Rosalee Win a Date with Tad Hamilton and Save the Children."

Rosalee smiled as she rang up a customer's order, because behind her, she could hear Cathy asking, "Would you like paper or plastic?" and "Would you like to help Rosalee win a date with Tad Hamilton and save the children?"

If everyone at the store right now contributed a little something, she'd have her hundred dollars in no time.

Mr. Ruddy held out a wooden plaque to Pete. It looked familiar. It looked just like the forty-three other ones he already had on the wall.

This is getting redundant, Pete thought as Mr. Ruddy handed him a check. *And embarrassing.*

"Along with a check for a hundred and twenty-five dollars in recognition of yet another Piggly Wiggly Store Manager of the Month Award. Congratulations."

Mr. Ruddy was so used to delivering this speech in this office that he said it quickly, and in a monotone, as if he were as bored with the procedure as Pete was.

"Thank you, Mr. Ruddy," Pete said.

Mr. Ruddy looked around the already-crowded walls for a place to put the newest plaque. "So, how long 'til you move to Richmond, Pete? You're running out of wall space here."

No kidding, thought Pete. He was running out of space in general. "Well, I got the acceptance letter from Virginia State, I got the student loan, so there's just…" Pete hesitated.

"What?" Mr. Ruddy prompted him.

"Oh, nothing, you know," Pete said. He didn't exactly want to discuss it with Mr. Ruddy. Talking about it with Mr. Ruddy would be like talking to his dad or something.

"Is there a girl involved?" Mr. Ruddy suddenly asked.

What was he, a mind reader now? Or was it that obvious to everyone else? "Why do you ask?" Pete said.

Mr. Ruddy shrugged. "There's always a girl involved."

Always? Pete thought. *Really?* "I just… there's someone I want to ask to go with me," he admitted.

"I didn't know you had a girlfriend, Pete." Mr. Ruddy looked at Pete's cluttered desk, as if he might find a photograph of this girl.

There weren't any pictures of her there. But in his apartment, there were a ton: Pete working with her at the freshman car wash, Pete with her at the senior prom (not that they went together as a couple, though), at high school graduation, at one of last year's Piggly Wiggly softball games. And that wasn't even counting all the other pictures of her. But that didn't mean Rosalee was his girlfriend—just one of his best friends.

"Well, she's not technically my girlfriend. As such. Per se," Pete heard himself babbling.

Mr. Ruddy looked confused. "Oh?"

There were three rapid knocks on the door, and without waiting for an answer, Rosalee walked in, carrying a couple of the "Win a Date" coin jars.

"Jars are full already! I love everyone who shops in this store," she said as she set the jars down on Pete's desk. Then she realized that Pete wasn't the only one in his office. She smiled at Mr. Ruddy. "Sorry to interrupt!" She quickly backed out of the office and closed the door behind her.

"Is that her?" Mr. Ruddy asked.

Pete nodded. "Yes."

Mr. Ruddy was obviously impressed—more like bowled over, as far as Pete could tell—by Rosalee's appearance. "Gee," he said, sounding a bit dumbfounded.

"I know," Pete said. *Believe me, I know.*

"Good-bye." Tad glanced at his watch as he hugged his latest date. They both smiled politely at each other before she went out to her car, and he closed the door behind her.

Tad turned around from his front door and adjusted the quilt he was wearing around his waist. She was nice, very nice. She was beautiful. Completely gorgeous. Fun. But would he miss her? No, not really.

Tad's housekeeper, Sonja, was getting ready to clock out for the day.

"Muchas gracias—hasta el próximo miércoles!" Tad said to her. It was the only Spanish that Tad knew, and he'd learned it from shooting a commercial. It meant, "Thank you. See you next Wednesday."

"I am the Albanian one, Mr. Hamilton," Sonja said.

Tad smacked his forehead lightly. "Oh, right, sorry. Please tell the other lady, *Muchas gracias— hasta el próximo miércoles!*"

Sonja smiled, but it was a cold smile, as if she was not all that amused by Tad. "Will do," she promised before leaving.

When the door closed, Tad could almost swear he heard an echo. His house was a little too empty right now. Tad went into the kitchen to get something for dinner. He opened the freezer and sorted through the healthy gourmet meals Sonja had prepared for him in advance. Each one was carefully wrapped and sealed, and had a bright Post-it note on it with the amount of time needed to cook it. Tad closed his eyes and picked one at random. He didn't really care what it was. He pushed it into the microwave and hit the button for five minutes.

Then he grabbed a bottle of Evian from the fridge and sat down on the sofa, clicking the remote for the plasma TV that hung on the wall. A family drama was on, and Tad settled down, getting comfortable among the dozen pillows on the sofa.

After a few minutes he thought: why was he watching this, a show that bore absolutely no relation to his life, a show with zero characters even remotely like him. On top of that, he couldn't even *think* about ever auditioning for a guest-star part on the show, not with his image the way it was these days.

Well, actually, maybe he could show up as the sad, disgruntled, fallen-from-grace actor who needed someone to give him a second chance. And the nice, sweet family would take him in. They'd have to.

But wait. Something was wrong with this picture. He was daydreaming about moving in with a fictional family. Wow. He definitely needed a change: his life was empty—totally empty—at times. Like now. There had to be more to life than microwaved meals and making out with models. Didn't there?

"Twenty-seven, twenty-seven-fifty…" Rosalee counted the money from the "Win a Date with Tad Hamilton" jars. She'd dumped all of the change onto Pete's desk and was sorting it into stacks. It had looked like so much, at first, when she brought the jars into the office. She would have guessed there was enough to enter the contest twice. But now? She was down to nickels, and it wasn't exactly looking promising. "Twenty-seven seventy-five," she counted.

"Eighteen, six, four, G, Bingo!" Pete interrupted her.

"Pete."

"It's twenty-eight forty," Pete told her.

"Not bad," Cathy commented.

"I'd say very generous. Nobody ever gave me a nickel to go out on a date," Pete said.

"It's for Save the Children," Rosalee reminded him.

"Don't say it like that, with that noble tone in your voice. You're just using those children to try to get to Tad Hamilton," Pete said accusingly. "If you were a child, is that the way you'd want to be saved?"

"No, you're right, Pete." Cathy rolled her eyes. "I'd turn down the inoculations on principle."

Rosalee was only half-listening to them, as she punched figures into the calculator on Pete's desk. "Add my entire suede jacket fund, Dad's early birthday gift, and yours as well, Cathy, thank you."

"You're welcome," Cathy said, with a smile.

"Make no mention of the total lack of participation from you, Pete…" Rosalee left the sentence unfinished, waiting for Pete's guilt to kick in. How could he not help her with this, when he knew how much it meant to her? That wouldn't be like Pete. That wasn't Pete.

"Matter of principle," Pete said again. He'd been saying that a lot lately. It was starting to annoy Rosalee—as if Pete had more principles than she did. "The whole transaction is on very shaky moral ground," Pete said.

Who cared about moral ground when she might get the chance to met Tad Hamilton? "I am twenty-seven dollars short," Rosalee concluded with a sigh. She turned around and looked at Pete with doleful, pleading eyes. Cathy did the same.

"Here we go." Pete sighed and opened the top right drawer of his desk. He pulled out the latest award check he'd received from Mr. Ruddy. "Cathy, take this up front and cash it for me, would you?"

Cathy smiled as she took the check from him. "Oh, you are a good and decent man."

"I love you!" Rosalee cried.

"Um, yes, great, cool." Pete shifted awkwardly. "But this in no way means I condone what you're doing. I'm just thinking of the *children*."

Rosalee nodded. "I understand." She turned to the computer on Pete's desk. "All righty. We are, I believe, ready."

"Good luck, doll!" Cathy called as she left the office to go cash the check.

"Yikes a bee." Rosalee took a deep breath, then clicked the box that said "Click Here to Enter."

CHAPTER **THREE**

"So what do I need to beat you?" Pete stood in front of the dartboard inside Li'l Dickens.

"Double fourteen, or it's all over," Rosalee told him.

"No problem," Pete said. He drew the back end of the dart toward his line of vision and lined up his shot. He'd been playing darts for years. He could hit almost any shot that he wanted to.

"Don't miss don't miss don't miss don't miss don't miss—" Rosalee chanted as Pete pumped his arm back and forth, focusing his aim one last time before throwing the dart.

Pete laughed and looked over at her. "Are you really doing that?" Sometimes he couldn't believe her. He didn't know whether to be charmed or annoyed.

She grinned and kept chanting. "Don't miss

don't miss, don't—"

"Unbelievable!" Pete muttered, smiling. He faked a dart toss, and Rosalee screamed, trying to psych him out as soon as he pretended to release the dart from his fingers. He looked over at her. "You are a shameless and, ironically, shame*ful* woman."

She was so competitive that she wasn't about to stop now. "Don't miss don't miss—" she continued.

Pete kept looking at her and aimed the dart at the board. He threw it without looking, and the dart just missed landing in the triple 14 ring. He'd lost. No double 14, no triple 14. Just…14.

"You buy the round!" Rosalee cried happily.

"Alllll right," Pete said with a sigh. Before walking over to the bar to join her and Cathy, he pulled a dart from the board and tossed it over his shoulder as he walked away. It landed directly in the double 14 this time.

Sure, he could have won. But what would be the point in that? He didn't mind buying the next round. He still had money left over from the latest "Manager of the Month" check he'd cashed. And since when had he ever minded treating Rosalee? Since never.

Pete slid onto a stool at the bar, where Cathy was already perched next to Rosalee.

"And now, Pete will get the bartendress's attention," Rosalee announced playfully.

Pete felt a lurch in the pit of his stomach. *I have no trouble getting Angelica's attention,* he thought as he glanced at the bartendress in question. *The problem is that I can't get rid of it.* For some reason, Angelica had decided that he, Pete Monash, was the man of her dreams. "Rosalee, why do you enjoy my pain so much?" he asked.

"I don't! I just happen to think that the two of you might make a very good match someday," Rosalee said.

"Yes. Someday when we're both completely different people," Pete argued.

Rosalee nudged his arm with her elbow. "She's waiting for you, pal."

"And we're waiting for our round," Cathy reminded him.

Pete sighed. "Fine." He cleared his throat and tried not to look interested in anything but a drink. "Angelica?" he said tentatively.

If a person behind a bar could move any faster, Pete would be surprised. He had barely finished saying her name, and there she was. "Yes, Pete? What is the object of your desire?" Angelica asked.

Someone in this room, thought Pete, *but not you.* "Uh, another round, please."

She smiled and started to pour their drinks. "One day, Pete, I know that the answer to that question will be, '*You,* Angelica. *You* are the object of my desire.'"

"Um, okay," Pete said, really wishing he could end this conversation. "But in the meantime, just the drinks?"

Angelica stared at him, pausing mid-pour. "My God, you are a handsome man."

"Th—uh—thank you," Pete stammered.

"Honestly, you have never looked hotter than you do at this moment." Angelica took a step forward to admire him, and Pete nearly fell off the back of the bar stool, straining to create a little distance between them.

Pete could feel Rosalee and Cathy staring at him, with huge smiles on their faces. They were loving this. "I, um… You know, I feel hot," he sputtered to Angelica.

An hour later, Cathy and Rosalee were still laughing as Pete drove them home in his old, slightly beat-up, slightly louder-than-is-technically-legal Ford Mustang.

"'My God, you are a handsome man!'" Rosalee exclaimed, quoting Angelica for what had to be the hundredth time. And then she and Cathy howled with laughter yet again.

"Okay, that's enough," Pete said.

Rosalee finally stopped laughing for a second. "You don't like her the littlest bit?" she asked.

Didn't she know the answer by now? "She's not my type, Rosie. For one thing, she's got too many tattoos," Pete complained. "A man's got to know where to focus."

Rosalee looked at him for a second, studying his expression. "You are so particular."

Pete decided to take that as a compliment. He turned down Rosalee's street, and as they got closer to her house, he slowed the Mustang. There was nowhere to park. The street was filled with extra cars, and TV news vans, and there was a clump of people wandering back and forth on the sidewalk. A couple of cameramen were milling around, followed by lighting people and reporters with microphones.

"Who the heck are they?" Cathy asked, leaning forward in the backseat.

"I swear, if that fire alarm went off again...." Rosalee mused.

Pete pulled over as close to the house as he could get.

"Holy smokes," Rosalee breathed. She flung open the Mustang's passenger-side door, nearly taking out a cameraman and a reporter wearing a suit who'd approached the car.

And then Rosalee was jumping up and down and screaming happily, and Pete knew.

She had done it. She had won a date with Tad Hamilton. And he had actually *helped.* How ironic was that?

CHAPTER **FOUR**

Rosalee was so nervous that she could hardly keep her composure. She kept expecting someone to walk up to her and tell her that this was all a joke, that she wasn't about to get on a plane and fly to Los Angeles to meet Tad Hamilton. Not just meet him—go on a date with him.

Beside her in the airport, Cathy sat listening for all the details Rosalee knew, even though they'd gone over and over them a dozen times since the night she found out she'd be going to Hollywood. And Pete was there to see her off, too, which was so sweet, except that he kept making digs at Tad Hamilton.

"They said that in the first-class cabin, you get a personal DVD player and may view the film of your choice," she told Cathy now.

"Okay, I would like to kiss the person who thought of that," Cathy said.

"What movies will you 'view'?" Pete asked.

"It's going to be a Tad Hamilton film festival," Rosalee said with a smile.

"There's a shock." Pete didn't bother to hide his sarcasm. Rosalee knew he still wasn't thrilled about the fact she was going to California to meet Tad Hamilton. But she was going. There was no getting around it.

"You can't fully appreciate his movies until the third or fourth viewing," Rosalee told him.

Pete smiled politely. "That explains it, then."

Rosalee held up the travel guide she'd picked up at the bookstore that morning. "And, I'm going to read up on all the must-sees in the fabulous City of Angels."

Cathy leaned forward in her chair and reached for the book. "I hear the Pacific Ocean is totally different from the Atlantic."

Pete rolled his eyes. "Yes, it's orange, actually."

Rosalee glanced over at the gate agent as he made an announcement welcoming everyone to the flight. "Ladies and gentlemen, at this time we'll begin boarding our first-class passengers," he said.

"That's *you!*" Cathy shrieked.

"I know!" Rosalee squealed.

Pete held his hands over his ears. "All right, easy there."

Rosalee got to her feet and swung her bag over her shoulder. "Oh, Petey, just gimme a hug and tell me to have a good time, would you please?"

Pete stood beside her, looking a bit worried. "You just be careful," he said.

"What do you mean?" Rosalee asked.

"I mean, the guy's *Tad Hamilton,*" Pete warned. "In his life, he's probably slept with like…fifteen or twenty women."

"No way," Rosalee scoffed. "That's not even physically possible. Besides—like Tad Hamilton's really going to be interested in me." *That was absurd, really,* she thought. They'd have about an hour to get to know each other. She didn't expect much more than a pleasant—and expensive—meal together.

"Here's how you'll know, okay? If at any point in the date, he claims that he doesn't really like watching sports? He's just trying to sleep with you," Pete said.

"Okay," Rosalee said, rolling her eyes. "Got it."

"And if he claims to love animals? He's *really* trying to sleep with you," Pete warned.

"Okay then, Pete." Rosalee started moving toward the open doorway leading to the Jetway. She wasn't sure she wanted to know much more about the way guys operated.

"Guys are guys, Rosalee. Rich or poor, famous or grocers," Pete explained.

"Uh huh."

"You just guard your carnal treasure there, Rosalee, okay?" Pete said, a little too loudly for Rosalee's taste. Everyone in the gate area—other passengers, the reporters and photographers, even the gate agent—was staring at her now. "You just guard it!" Pete continued.

Rosalee could feel her face turn red. "Yes, okay, thank you," she mumbled as she backed away a little.

Cathy followed her and reached out for a hug. "Remember everything," she said to Rosalee.

"I will," Rosalee promised.

"Remember how he smells," Cathy said, letting her go.

Rosalee nodded. "I will."

"But not just vaguely. I want good, solid similes," Cathy went on. "For example, 'He smells like a forest on the first day of spring, after a lightning storm, when—'"

"Cathy, she's gonna miss the plane," Pete interrupted her.

Rosalee smiled at her best friend. "I will bring you similes."

Cathy smiled, too. "Thank you."

Rosalee picked up her small carry-on suitcase and headed toward the open doorway, holding out her boarding pass to the agent. Just as she was handing it over, Pete called after her, "Just guard that carnal treasure!"

Rosalee glanced over her shoulder at him, noticing that everyone was still staring at her. "I *heard* you!" she called back to him. Then she waved, smiled, and headed down the Jetway.

"Do I have to go?" Tad knew he was sort of whining, but he couldn't help himself. This dumb publicity stunt hadn't been his idea. He wanted that noted for the record.

"It'll be perfectly painless," his agent Richard assured him from inside Tad's gigantic walk-in bedroom closet. Richard was choosing an outfit for Tad to wear that night.

Tad's manager held up one of Tad's thirty pairs of Nike sneakers. "Can I have these?"

"It's already not painless," Tad complained to his agent. "Tell me again why you're making me have dinner with an Okie?"

"Because she's wholesome." His agent examined a shirt and pants combination. "And she's not an Okie. She's from West Virginia."

Tad knew he should recognize the distinction, but he didn't. And he didn't exactly care about that fact. "Sorry," he said.

Tad's manager was still obsessing over the sneakers. Now he was trying them on and admiring himself in one of the full-length mirrors. "You never wear them. I've never seen you wear them. Can I have them?" he asked.

"What's her name, anyway?" Tad asked, ignoring him. He was too annoyed by this concept of a forced, prearranged date.

"Rosalee Futch," his agent said with a smile.

Tad could only imagine. Her name rhymed with

"hutch." That couldn't be good. "Sounds insanely hot," he commented dryly.

"Just follow the rules—"

Tad repeated the familiar refrain along with his agent. "Keep smiling for the cameras, and no brown liquor or cigarettes." Tad sighed. "Fine. Did we hear from Jimmy Ing yet?"

His agent shook his head rapidly. "No."

"Because I passed Ashton Kutcher in a car, and he looked really happy about *something*." That might mean Jimmy Ing had given him the part. Then again, Ashton Kutcher had a thousand reasons to be happy. Tad, however, did not.

"We have not heard from him," his agent said meaningfully. Which meant that there was no way Tad was getting out of this date. He needed it, for his image.

His manager had abandoned the Nikes now and was trying on an expensive Italian suit jacket. "How is this in the shoulders?" he asked, turning back and forth in front of Tad.

Rosalee sat in her deluxe hotel room, perched on the king-sized bed. She'd never stayed at such a nice hotel before. She had a suite and every luxury in the world: a gigantic bath tub, various beauty products, towels bigger than her sheets back home, a mini bar stocked to the hilt with snacks and fancy drinks.

She'd gotten ready for the date a little on the

early side—three hours early, to be exact. Which meant she'd been obsessing about Tad Hamilton, and her dress, and her hair, and everything remotely connected to this evening, for three straight hours.

"It's very nice to meet you, Tad." She paused, thinking about whether that sounded right. "So nice to meet you, Tad," she said. No, that wasn't it, either. "Great to meet you." There. Perfect. *Great to meet you,* she thought, repeating the phrase so that she would get it right when she finally saw him. *Great to meet you.*

Then there would be the little matter of ordering dinner correctly. Rosalee had to think about that. "I'll have the soft shell crabs," she rehearsed. "I think, Tad, that I will have the soft shell crabs."

She shifted on the bed, propping a pillow more carefully so that it wouldn't wrinkle her dress. What else was she going to say to him?

"Your films will stand the test of *time,*" she said out loud. Or maybe, "*Your* films will stand the test of time." She thought for a second. *Which word should she emphasize most?* "Your films will *stand* the test of time."

Rosalee gasped as the room doorbell suddenly rang. She was so startled that for a second she forgot what she was supposed to do, but then she shut her eyes and mouthed her greeting one last time. Taking a deep breath, she stood up and opened the door.

Tad Hamilton was standing there, looking incredibly handsome He smiled at her, and she nearly fell over. "Hi. I'm Tad."

Rosalee smiled back at him, and in a shaking voice said, "Your standing films will test and time themselves."

"Uh, thank you," Tad replied, a bit confused. "You're very pretty."

Rosalee coughed, so overwhelmed that she nearly keeled over. She was glad she was still holding onto the door, that she hadn't yet invited him into the room, because she needed to hold on to the handle for dear life. Tad Hamilton had just said she, Rosalee Futch, was "very pretty."

She could die now.

Except that she'd miss the date.

CHAPTER **FIVE**

"It's Roseanne, right?" Tad asked, looking concerned.

Rosalee shook her head. She wasn't sure she was ready to try talking again. She'd blown it the first time, and now he'd complimented her and she was completely out of oxygen.

Tad seemed to focus on her face a little more while he waited for her to speak. "I'm sorry—what is it?" he pressed.

Rosalee waved at him, trying to tell him it was unimportant. He'd called her "pretty." Did he need to do any better than that?

"Come on," he said. "Rosalyn?" She shook her head again. "Rosamund?" he guessed.

Clearly he wasn't going to get this on his own. "Rosalee," she finally managed to croak.

"Rosalee," he repeated.

She nodded.

"You ready?" Tad asked.

She nodded again. It seemed to be the only thing she was good at when he was around.

"Good." Tad smiled and held the door open while she walked out into the hallway. She couldn't take her eyes off of him. The way he closed the door...it was so cool, so effortless, so magical somehow. She felt as if they were in a movie together, something romantic and black-and-white.

Then she realized she'd left her purse inside. Just before the lock latched, she pushed open the door and rushed inside to grab her sweater and purse. She came back out with an embarrassed smile.

He walked beside her down the hallway, and a security guard she hadn't noticed at first fell into step behind them. She couldn't stop staring at Tad, his jaw line, his perfect strong cheekbones, his wonderfully handsome face.

"So, how was the flight?" Tad asked.

She knew she was supposed to answer him. She knew that words were supposed to come out of her mouth right now. "Your films will stand the test of time," she finally said, a bit breathlessly.

"Oh." Tad nodded, as if he now understood what she'd been trying to express for the past five minutes. "Thanks. Are you ready?" Tad asked.

"For what?" Rosalee replied.

Tad didn't answer her. He just grinned as they

rounded the corner into the lobby, where a crowd of reporters, photographers, and curious onlookers were sitting—and standing—in wait for them. Camera bulbs flashed in Rosalee's eyes, and a hail of questions came at Tad. Rosalee noticed everyone in the entire hotel seemed to have stopped whatever they were doing to check out Tad—the desk clerks, the bellhops, the arriving guests—*everyone.*

The two of them hustled outside to the long, black limousine that was waiting for them. Rosalee slid onto a comfy leather seat along the side of the limo, and the driver closed the door behind them, sealing off the loud voices and bright lights.

"Is it always like that?" Rosalee asked Tad as the car started away from the hotel.

"Pretty much." Tad lit a cigarette and leaned back in the seat, looking relaxed.

Rosalee shook her head in disbelief. "Shake-a-doo."

Tad laughed at her. "What?"

Oh, no. Had she really just used that goofy Fraziers Bottom expression? "It just means… 'wow,'" she explained.

"Oh." Tad nodded. "Shake-a-doo," he said, trying it out for himself and seeming to like the sound of it.

She looked at him and tried to smile, but she was suddenly feeling a little bit sick. She could feel her forehead getting damp with sweat, and as she looked sideways across the car, the passing landscapes made her feel dizzy and faint.

"So, you excited?" Tad asked.

"Are you kidding?" Rosalee took a deep breath and attempted to steady herself. "This is like a fairy tale." *Except for the extreme nausea part.* Cinderella didn't turn green when Prince Charming showed up.

Tad was staring at her now, looking a little worried. "You okay?"

"Oh, yeah," Rosalee lied. "It's just…kind of funny sitting sideways like this. We don't have sideways seating in West Virginia. And then, the cigarette smoke…" She glanced at Tad, hoping he'd take the hint and extinguish his.

But he didn't seem to register her comment. "Would you like to come back here?" Tad offered, patting the seat beside him.

Rosalee would have liked nothing more, but it was too late. There was no way she could stand or even scoot at the moment. "I, uh, can't really move right now," she told Tad nervously.

"You can't?" Tad asked.

"I've always been sort of motion sickness-y," Rosalee quickly confessed. "Once, this carnival came to Fraziers Bottom, and they had that ride where you stand against the side and it spins around and the center falls out, and I… uh…" *Oh, no. Please no.* "Pardon me!" Rosalee managed to get up before she threw up in the corner of the limo.

Tad's eyes widened. So this was what a date with an ordinary citizen was all about. Was this what the Richard Levys thought would repair his damaged image? Tending to motion-sickness victims?

Maybe he'd send Rosalee Futch home in a cab—by herself. That way she could face forward, and if she felt the slightest bit ill...well, he wouldn't have to be there, he thought as he eyed her nervously. He'd handed her a box of breath mints and a hot washcloth, which fortunately he carried in a little compartment in the backseat. Having a fully stocked limo was handy like that.

The thing was she was almost beautiful enough to get away with puking in a limo. She was just one of those delicate-flower-type people. Tad didn't know very many of those. He knew more of the aggressive flowers. The Venus flytrap–types.

Fortunately they pulled up outside the Ivy restaurant about two minutes after the nauseous episode. Tad got out of the limo, and waited while the driver held out a hand to Rosalee to help her out.

The three of them stood on the curb for a second, waiting for Rosalee to get her bearings. She had been apologizing over and over again ever since the incident.

"This is just so far from the way I imagined the evening going," she said as she put another mint into her mouth.

"No, hey, it's perfectly all right," Tad assured her. "Right, Mickey?"

His driver frowned as he looked inside the back of the limo. "Perfectly all right," he said in a monotone.

"It's very refreshing. It's the first time I've ever seen a woman throw up *before* she eats," Tad joked. Then he leaned over and said quietly to Mickey, "Let's have it detailed."

"Believe me," Mickey replied.

Tad turned to Rosalee. "Do you still feel like a meal?"

"I do, actually," she said with a sweet smile.

So far he'd been surprised by her a couple of times. He sort of liked that. "Okay, then. Shall we?" He smiled and gestured toward the restaurant.

Five minutes later, they had been seated at the best, most exposed table in the Ivy—it was an outside table, on the porch. Tad noticed a few photographers standing on the Robertson Boulevard sidewalk, straining to get a good shot of him, to capture this sweet moment for their readers. *Well, that is the point of this whole night—to get good press,* Tad thought as he smiled his most charming smile for them. *Better not blow this, or I'll have to go through it again, with another girl from God-knows-where.*

Rosalee looked up from her menu, which she'd been studying. "Doesn't that hurt, smiling like that all the time?" she asked him.

Tad shrugged. "You get used to it."

Rosalee glanced at the news people, who were still watching their every move. "Should *I* do it?" she asked.

"You might not be able to hold it very long," Tad warned. This had taken him years to perfect, after all.

"Sure I will," Rosalee said confidently.

If the girl wanted to feel pain for some strange reason, then this would be a good time for it. "Okay. Then go ahead."

He watched, amused, as she smiled gamely for the photographers. She had a terrific smile, really. He was impressed. But after a minute or two, it looked like she was getting uncomfortable. Then she was clenching her jaw. And then her smile turned into a scary-looking scowl.

"That's horrible!" she said as she gave up and rubbed her cheeks.

Tad laughed. "I told you." He reached into his jacket pocket and took out his usual assortment of stuff: his keys, his cell phone, his cigarettes and lighter, and his Blackberry. He laid them on the table beside his bread plate.

Rosalee eyed the pile of things suspiciously. "Don't you have any pockets?"

"Sorry. I have to make sure I'm never out of touch with the people who torture and torment me," Tad said.

"Who are they?"

"Oh, agents, managers, this man Jimmy Ing who's making a movie that I'm exactly right for, but for some reason he's taking a breath," Tad told her.

Rosalee raised her eyebrows. "He's what?"

"He's thinking it over," Tad explained.

"Oh." Rosalee nodded.

Tad glared at the assortment of stuff. "I hate these things. This little digital, electronic army of pain." He saluted them all. "At ease!"

"I think the square one just laughed at you," Rosalee said.

Tad smiled in appreciation. He was stressed out, over nothing, over the way his phone wasn't ringing—she was right. "Sorry," he said. "It's just so competitive, this business. People don't realize. Everyone's chasing the same thing. The same parts in the same movies, the same awards, the big money…"

"Well, I'm sure you've got much too much common sense to get caught up in that nonsense," Rosalee told him. There was a certain confidence in her voice, as if she really believed in Tad, in this part of him that even he'd sort of lost track of and forgotten about. He sat up straighter in his chair as she went on, "I mean, that is a recipe for an unsatisfying life. But obviously, you've got your priorities straight."

Tad just stared at Rosalee, impressed. She saw through all the superficial crap. She was someone who took things a little more seriously—he'd underestimated her.

She smiled as she looked across the table at him. "What?"

"Nothing, nothing." Tad shook his head. "So, Rosalee. What do you do?"

"I work in a Piggly Wiggly."

A what? Tad thought. "I'm sorry?" he asked.

"A supermarket," Rosalee said.

"Oh." It wasn't what Tad expected. She seemed much too...*pretty* for that. Then again, he hadn't been to an actual supermarket in years. Maybe they were full of good-looking women.

"I bag and check," Rosalee added.

"Cool."

"Yeah. It's a dream come true," Rosalee said sarcastically. "But it's fun, actually. My two best friends work there." There was a brief, awkward pause, and then she asked, "So, um, what do you do, Tad?"

She started to laugh. "Oops. Stupid question."

She had a really nice laugh, Tad thought. It was genuine, and unforced. He didn't hear lots of laughs like that anymore.

Rosalee pushed a strand of hair off of her face as she smiled at him. "What do you do when you're not...you know. Being a movie star?"

"Not a lot, you know—there's not much time left for hobbies. And I don't really like watching sports, so..." He glanced at Rosalee, who had stopped smiling for some reason. When he paused, though, she started smiling again. "I read, I play with my dog, and my cat, and my bird," Tad explained. "I love animals." Again, Rosalee's smile disappeared. What was he doing wrong, he wondered. Was his non-movie-star life too boring for her?

A waiter finally approached the table. "What can I start you off with?" he asked.

"I'll have the soft shell crab, please, and then the fried chicken," Rosalee announced.

Tad sat back in his seat. This woman had an appetite unlike anyone he'd met. Since when did a beautiful, slender woman order fried chicken for dinner? An actress or model ordering fried anything was like Superman ordering Kryptonite.

"Okay," the waiter said. "But a drink to begin, or…?"

"Oh." Rosalee's face turned red, and Tad realized she was a bit out of her element. He should have helped her, he thought. "Uh…wine?" Rosalee asked.

"What kind?" The waiter waited for her to name something more specific.

"Uh, do you have cherry?" Rosalee asked.

"Cherry wine? Uh, sadly, no." The waiter gave her a cursory smile.

Rosalee looked up at him. "Well, uh, what do you suggest?"

"Give us a bottle of the Chateauneuf du Pape, if you would," Tad spoke up.

The waiter nodded. "Very good." Then he briskly disappeared.

Rosalee looked at Tad. "Thank you. I'm not good at wine. Fraziers Bottom is sort of a Boone's Farm kind of town."

Boone's Farm. Tad hadn't thought about that in years. When he was a teenager, that was what everyone tried to sneak from their parents' liquor cabinet. "I remember Boone's Farm!" he told her.

Rosalee's eyes widened in surprise. "You do?"

"Used to *love* the cherry," Tad said.

"The cherry's good," Rosalee agreed. "You ever have the apple?"

Tad shook his head. She was so cute. "Never had the apple."

"The apple's unbelievable. You have the apple, you may never go back to the cherry," Rosalee predicted.

Tad grinned. "I will have to try it."

"But, I *knew* they wouldn't have the apple," she joked.

Tad laughed. Who was this Rosalee Futch, anyway? He'd been dreading this date, but it was turning out to be better with every passing minute. Not that a date that started out with motion sickness could get worse, but still. She was beautiful, and funny, and she had that sort of honest clear-headedness that he never ran into anymore.

If he weren't Tad Hamilton, he could really fall for her.

CHAPTER **SIX**

Pete stared at the empty dartboard at Li'l Dickens. Just a few nights ago he'd been playing darts with Rosalee, throwing the game just so she could win, and so that he could buy her a drink. Now what? Now he was killing time with Cathy until Rosalee came home from California. He was sitting at the bar picturing Rosalee with Tad the Cad Hamilton.

"What do you suppose they're doing right now?" Pete asked Cathy. He couldn't help himself. He was sick.

"I bet they're in her hotel room, straining for breath, his manhood yearning to be free, her hands running over the ripples in his abdomen, her perfect bosom crying out in ecstasy," Cathy said.

Ask a stupid question, Pete thought as he frowned at her. Especially from someone who read way too many romance novels. "Great," he muttered.

Angelica came over to stand right in front of him, as if his night couldn't get any worse. "Hi, Pete," she said.

"Hi, Angelica." He tried to sound as unenthused as possible. He didn't want to lead her on—not that she needed any encouragement, apparently.

"How are you?" Angelica asked.

"Fine," Pete said blandly.

She picked a kernel of popcorn out of the bowl on the bar and, while staring at him, started to daintily eat the tiny corners off of it. Then she put the kernel on her tongue and drew it into her mouth, giving Pete a seductive look as she did.

This was all wrong. Angelica wanted him—badly—and he didn't want her. He wanted Rosalee.

"I have to go," Pete announced. He slid off the bar stool and headed for the door. "Something is wrong with the women in this town," he muttered as he headed across the parking lot toward his Mustang.

Rosalee took another sip of wine as Tad laughed at the latest detail from her afternoon. She was hilariously describing the tour of L.A. she'd taken when she got into town, and all the ridiculous things she'd seen while being driven around in a limo. She'd taken a tour of stars' homes, but all she'd seen were the stars' gardeners and groundskeepers, blowing leaves from their lawns into the street.

"And I thought, what planet is Los Angeles on? Actually driving the car is an afterthought, and nobody ever heard of a rake," she was saying as the waiter walked up carrying two plates.

"Soft shell crabs, grilled salad," the waiter said as he set them down on the table.

Tad and Rosalee both thanked him. "I just need a nutcracker when you get a chance, sir," Rosalee told him.

He indicated the plate of crabs in front of her. "Uh, ma'am, I think you'll enjoy it more just with a fork and knife."

"Oh. Right. Thanks," she said to the waiter. After he walked away, she looked sheepishly at Tad. "Forgot they were soft shell. Thought they were...regular shell."

"Oh, no, sure." Tad didn't care about her little mistakes. She wasn't used to all this. So what if she goofed now and then? It was adorable.

"All righty, then." Rosalee daintily reached into her mouth and pulled a retainer off of her lower teeth. She set it neatly on the table, beside her water glass.

For a moment, Tad stared in disbelief. He'd never known anyone remotely like her before. There was a certain charm to the way Rosalee just did everything without asking, with no self-consciousness.

She had a confidence that was attractive.

"I had one of those," Tad suddenly remembered.

"A retainer?" Rosalee asked.

"On the lowers, and a night brace on the uppers. I had really bad teeth as a kid." He wasn't sure why he was telling her this. It was just that her style was so disarming. He suddenly wanted to be completely open and honest with her.

Rosalee rolled her eyes. "Yeah, I'm sure you were a real ugly duckling."

"I was like anyone else," Tad admitted honestly. "A little gawky. Unsure who I was. Combination skin."

"Well, you came together nicely," Rosalee said, gazing at him.

"Thanks. So did you." He grinned at her.

She smiled, blushing a little.

"Bon appetit!" Tad reached for his salad fork and watched as Rosalee gingerly cut into her soft shell crab.

"Son of a gun," he heard her whisper.

He couldn't help smiling at her innocent expression. *Son of a gun. Shake-a-doo.* Where had she come from?

He looked at the cute way that little tendrils of Rosalee's soft, blond hair fell against her cheek. Shake-a-doo, indeed.

"Slow enough for you?" Tad asked.

Rosalee looked out the window as the limo

cruised down Mulholland Drive after dinner. They were sitting next to each other now, and facing forward this time, which was much better, she thought. "Perfect," Rosalee told Tad.

Tad opened a little door, revealing a wall-mounted bar. "Would you like a drink?" he offered.

"In the actual moving car?" Rosalee asked.

Tad stopped, his hand on a clean glass. "Why not?"

"I don't know." Rosalee wrinkled her nose. "Just seems like you're asking for it."

"You're right." Tad shut the bar compartment and instead reached for his cigarettes.

Rosalee stared at him in disbelief. Didn't he remember what happened last time he lit up in a moving car?

She noticed Mickey, the limo driver, glance at Tad in the rearview mirror, too. He definitely didn't want his limo to be puked in more than once in one day.

"Oh, right, right." Tad grinned and put the pack of cigarettes back into his suit jacket pocket. He looked out the window as they came to the top of a hill. "I want you to see this," he told Rosalee. Then he called forward, "Mickey, pull us over, would you?"

The limo turned off the road onto a scenic overlook, and Rosalee followed Tad out of the limo. They stood at the top of a canyon, with the valley spread out below them. Rosalee couldn't get over the thousands—no, millions—of tiny lights beneath them, the glittering city of Los Angeles. It was a long, long way from Fraziers Bottom—and about a billion times more populated.

"Wow," Rosalee commented.

Tad nodded in agreement.

"Boy, these people sure leave a lot of lights on." She scanned the valley, admiring the view. "It's beautiful."

"It is," Tad agreed. He turned toward Rosalee, stepping closer to her. "And you, if I may say so, are also beautiful," he added.

Rosalee looked up at him, and she let out a small laugh. "You gotta stop saying stuff like that, okay?"

"Why?" Tad countered. "It's true."

"No, it's not," Rosalee said. "And even if it were, you gotta stop saying it."

"Okay." Tad smiled, and gazed out at the view for a moment. Rosalee wasn't sure what she should do or say next. The evening wasn't quite over yet—she wanted it to last a while longer.

Then Tad asked, "Would you like to come back to the house for a little while?"

Rosalee thought about Pete's warnings. She remembered Tad saying that he didn't like to watch sports on TV, which was, according to Pete, a bad sign. And then Tad had said how much he loved animals, just like Pete had warned.

But so what? Pete wasn't here. She didn't like

watching sports and she did love animals, and that didn't make *her* a bad person, did it?

"Sure," she told Tad, not feeling sure at all. "For a little while."

I can't wait to tell Cathy about this! That was the first thought Rosalee had when she walked into Tad's house. *I am in Tad Hamilton's house. She's not going to believe this. I don't believe this!*

"Shake-a-doo?" Tad asked as they paused in the front foyer.

She nodded eagerly; she was speechless. She'd never seen a house like this before. She'd never seen a house this *large* before, actually—unless barns counted.

"Good."

"I mean, you know, it's not exactly my taste," Rosalee heard herself babble. What was she talking about? The place was amazing, incredible, fantastic. The only other time she'd seen anything like this was a feature about Tad in a magazine—when he lived in his old place, a slightly smaller mansion, before his latest box-office smash.

"Mrs. Ramirez? Sonja?" Tad called into the house. "Anybody in the casa?"

They both stood in the foyer and waited for an answer, but heard nothing.

"I think we're all alone," Tad said as he started to move into the house.

"Oh." Rosalee was momentarily stunned. She was alone with Tad Hamilton, in his house. And all of a sudden she couldn't move her feet, she couldn't follow him.

"Would you like to…come farther in?" Tad asked.

Rosalee looked at him. If she walked into the house now, she might do something she'd regret. She didn't usually go to a guy's place on a first date. And even though this was the first date of a lifetime…she still had to stick to her rules.

"You know what, Tad, thank you, but I think I should be getting back to the hotel. I don't want the concierge to worry," Rosalee said, trying to make light of the situation.

"Really? Wow." Tad looked very surprised and maybe, Rosalee thought, slightly impressed. He probably didn't experience this very often. "Good for you," Tad said. "Come on—I'll take you back," he offered.

"Oh, no, you don't have to do that. You're home already," Rosalee pointed out.

Tad smiled—that charming, devastatingly seductive smile that made Rosalee want to change her mind and *sprint* into the house. "It'll be my pleasure," he said.

"Okay. That's really nice."

The limo pulled up in front of the Peninsula Hotel, and Tad turned to Rosalee. She couldn't believe this incredible night was over. She wished it could happen all over again, in slow motion—and this time without the getting-sick part.

Tad smiled at her, and it was that same, melt-your-heart smile she knew from his movies, but now she knew what it felt like to have him look that way at *her.* "Rosalee, it's been wonderful to meet you," Tad said. "I wish you only good things in life."

"And to me, wonderfulness, too, and to you, those only good self-same wishes." Rosalee heard herself talking, and she knew what she was trying to express, but it wasn't coming out right. *Don't blow it now, Rosalee,* she thought. *This is the last time you'll ever be alone with Tad Hamilton.* "You know what I'm saying. Thank you for the best night of my life."

"Thank you. May I give you a kiss good-bye?" Tad asked.

He was so polite, it was killing her. "Oh, I think you might maybe may..." she said slowly.

Tad leaned over and pressed his lips to hers. Rosalee held her breath as she kissed him back. It was the most fantastic kiss she'd ever experienced. It was a good thing she was sitting down, because she could swear she felt her knees buckle.

Then Tad slowly pulled away from her, keeping his hand lightly touching her cheek. He looked into her eyes and Rosalee literally squeaked with pleasure.

Tad smiled at the tiny sound, and Rosalee had to force herself to take Mickey's offered hand and step out of the limo. She thanked him and then walked in a daze from the limo to the hotel lobby door. She was so happy that she wasn't sure if she wanted to laugh, or scream, or cry first.

Keep it together, Rosalee, she told herself as she walked through the lobby, nodding politely at the hotel staff. *Don't make a complete idiot of yourself.* She stood silently in the elevator with other passengers, still containing her excitement. She felt like a can of Coke that had been shaken violently, like she would explode as soon as she opened her mouth.

She made it to her suite and closed the door behind her. Then she burst into laughter and jumped onto the bed, then onto the floor, where she spun around and did a somersault.

Suddenly she found herself staring at a pair of feet in uniform support-style black shoes.

Rosalee gazed up from the floor.

"Turn-down service?" the maid offered politely.

Rosalee grinned at her, not even feeling embarrassed. "Please."

CHAPTER SEVEN

Pete sat at his desk in his Piggly Wiggly office, listening to Rosalee's tale of Hollywood. She had started telling him and Cathy about it nearly half an hour ago. Their lunch break was nearly over—the story had taken as long as the actual date itself. Although for Pete it was twice as painful in the telling.

She looks different, he thought as he looked at her. He didn't know what it was, but she looked different.

However, one thing hadn't changed. She still had the ability to discuss Tad Hamilton *ad nauseum.* Why hadn't the so-called actor been a jerk on the date? Why did he have to win her over even more by *kissing* her? That was overkill, Pete thought bitterly.

"Mickey opened the limo door," Rosalee went on.

"My foot hit the ground and I turned to take one last look at Tad. At those eyes. At that smile. Then, regretfully, I started for the hotel." Rosalee gazed into space, a glassy expression in her eyes. Cathy was lost in a dream world as well—she was staring at the coffee table as if it were a crystal ball that would give her answers.

"Please tell me we're done now," Pete said to break the annoying mood.

"We're done," Rosalee said, seeming depressed about that fact.

"I cannot remember a time before you started telling that story," Pete added.

"Peter, I was asked to provide a detailed description of the evening," Rosalee said in self-defense.

"And you did a great job, Rosie. Really—I feel like I was there. Sort of against my will," Pete told her. "And now, with your permission, perhaps we can all return to our lives?"

Rosalee let out a loud sigh. "Okay."

Pete cleared his throat. He couldn't believe he was about to do this, but he was—he'd made up his mind while she was away worshiping Tad Hamilton in person. He walked over to the coffee table to get closer to Rosalee. "Especially because, Rosie, I have something very important to tell you."

Cathy leaned forward on the sofa, as if she were going to be a part of the conversation. That wasn't what Pete had in mind. He gave her a look, and Cathy sank back on the sofa.

"Something I think you'll like," Pete continued. "At least, I hope you'll like it." *I really, really hope that. One could say "desperately."* Pete glared at Cathy again. Couldn't she tell that he and Rosalee needed some privacy? She moved over to the end of the sofa and picked up a magazine. Pete wished she would leave, but he didn't want Rosalee to get suspicious. Anyway, this was his moment—he couldn't lose it. He looked at Rosalee, who was waiting for him with a quizzical expression in her eyes.

"It's been a long time coming," Pete said nervously. "It may come as a surprise. Or it may not. But it may." Pete rubbed his neck—it seemed as if the words were getting stuck in his throat. "Sorry—I'm a little nervous. But, okay, I'm ready. What I have to say to you is—"

The office door swung open and Pete glanced up, annoyed, expecting to see Janine or Herb asking if they could have a long lunch.

Instead, Tad Hamilton was standing there, smiling from ear to ear, beaming as if he'd just won the lottery.

His timing in real life was atrocious, in Pete's opinion. "Okay, what would be the absolute worst thing that could happen right now?" he asked.

"Huh?" Rosalee looked confused. She hadn't yet seen Tad, because her back was to the door.

Meanwhile, Cathy was holding out the uneaten

Rosalee and Pete discuss the megastar.

Strategy time with the Richard Levys.

Tad is so fantastic!

"Shake-a-doo!"

Tad and Pete get acquainted.

The girl from Fraziers Bottom, West Virginia.

Rosalee's dad talks shop with Tad.

Tad Hamilton tries to get his priorities straight
as half the population of Fraziers Bottom looks on.

Inside Li'l Dickens, Rosalee and Tad are an item.

Rosalee gets a ride on Tad's private jet.

Rosalee and Pete thinking about their true feelings . . .

Alone with Tad . . .

Alone with Pete . . .

Which one will she choose?

half of her tuna sandwich. "You can have this if you want."

"What?" Rosalee asked.

"Turn around," Pete told her.

But she still wasn't getting it. Cathy gestured for her to turn around and urgently pointed over Rosalee's shoulder. Slowly, excruciatingly slowly as far as Pete was concerned, Rosalee turned.

"Hi," Tad Hamilton said, his face lighting up.

Rosalee didn't move. "No way," she said breathlessly.

Tad glanced at Pete and then at Cathy. "Hi. I'm Tad," he said.

Duh, Pete thought. And did he have to be so polite? He didn't trust anyone who was *that* polite. He also didn't trust anyone who tracked someone down at work in a completely different state. That was just plain weird.

"Uh, this is my Cathy friend," Rosalee said, completely flustered. She got to her feet and gestured toward Cathy.

"Hello," Cathy said in a somewhat husky voice.

"And my Pete friend," Rosalee added.

Pete held out his hand to shake Tad's. "Quite pleased and pleasant to make your know." He shook his head. What had he just babbled?

"I've heard a lot about you both," Tad said with a grin.

"Have you?" Cathy asked.

Pete muttered something. Sometimes he really wished that he could just stop himself from talking.

"What, uh…what are you doing here?" Rosalee asked Tad.

Finally, Pete thought. He wanted to know about that himself.

"I came to see you," Tad said, as if it were completely obvious, which it basically was.

But that hadn't exactly been the answer Pete wanted to hear. Still, he knew there could be no other reason Tad Hamilton decided to just drop by the Fraziers Bottom Piggly Wiggly.

"No way," Rosalee said. "You're just…that's just…you can't, it's like…" she stammered.

Tad gave her a cute little punch on the shoulder. "It's true!"

"You mean to say your normal business itinerary does not include Fraziers Bottom, West Virginia?" Cathy asked him in a heavy Southern accent Pete hadn't heard from her before.

"Hey, Blanche DuBois—why don't you give it a rest," Rosalee said.

"Can I not make some pleasant banter with a stranger?" Cathy replied in a soft, breathy voice.

"Okay, Cath."

"So." Tad stepped closer to Rosalee. "Am I too late to take you to lunch?"

Yes, Pete thought. *Way too late. We already had lunch, and she's already eaten, and I was just about to tell her something very, very important, so obviously she can't go now.*

"N-no. Not at all," Rosalee said. Pete watched as she swept her empty sandwich bag, empty soup bowl, empty Pringles can, and discarded candy-bar wrapper off the desk toward the garbage can. Usually he'd push the can right under the falling trash, but he was too discombobulated now to move. The wrappers and bowl and can bounced as they hit the linoleum floor. Nobody even seemed to notice, besides Pete.

"Great," Tad said, ignoring the mess. "Shall we?"

"Um, sure. If it's *okay,* Pete?" Rosalee asked.

"Well, actually…" Pete stalled. It wasn't okay. And did she expect him to clean up this mess?

"If it is okay, *Pete,*" Rosalee said, more firmly this time, as if she were demanding his permission instead of requesting it. Then she gave him The Look, which she reserved for other important times when she wanted to strangle him.

"Okay," Pete agreed. "I'll put you back on at two."

"At which point, Tad, if you're headed back to the airport, I will ride with you," Cathy offered.

"*Cathy,*" Rosalee scolded.

"Hey, you want a shy girl? Go by the church," Cathy said with a shrug.

"Um, it was very nice to meet you both," Tad said to both of them.

"Uh, yeah," Pete mumbled. He wished he could say the same.

"Oh, yes," Cathy whispered.

Rosalee picked up her purse and was about to open the door when she turned around. "Oh, Pete—did you have something you were going to say before?" she asked.

Not just something, Pete thought. *Everything.* "Uh, no," he muttered. Why did he feel like his life was suddenly taking a drastic, horrible turn?

Tad opened the office door and nearly got flattened by all of the people pressed against it, eavesdropping. Two customers fell to the floor in front of him, pushed by the crowd behind them.

"All right, nothing to see here," Rosalee said to everyone. "Go back to your…aisles."

Rosalee and Tad headed for the exit—the crowd following them like a golf-course gallery. Pete followed them, too, and stood at the front of the store, watching them exit to the parking lot out front, watching as Tad held the passenger door of his rental car open for Rosalee.

Pete suddenly sensed Cathy standing next to him, watching him watch *them.* "And that was the last time we ever saw her," she joked.

"Relax, Cath. He's not her type," Pete declared.

She shook her head. "Oh, no. Handsome, rich, famous—you're absolutely right."

Pete frowned at her. "What I mean is, the guy's a mess." Had she forgotten every tabloid story she'd read and insisted on reading to him?

"Right, and women are *never* attracted to that," she said.

Pete looked at Cathy. She was right. He had no chance, no chance at all. He felt his hopes for him and Rosalee ever being a couple completely evaporating, right there at checkout lane 2. "All right, so, fine, so even if she goes for him, you think it's gonna last forever?" he asked Cathy.

She shrugged. "No."

"No—he'll lose interest in ten or several minutes," Pete declared.

"Doesn't matter. Our Rosie was not built for short and inconsequential affairs, Pete. She does things with her whole heart or not at all. So if he's with her forever, you lose her forever, and if he's with her for ten or several minutes and then he dumps her, she'll never be the same and you lose her forever," Cathy said.

Pete thought about it for a second. She was so right. "You're so annoying," he said.

Now what was he going to do?

CHAPTER **EIGHT**

Rosalee couldn't believe the scene at the diner. Apparently nothing this exciting had ever happened in Fraziers Bottom before. She could hardly blame the people who were crowded around the plate-glass window, watching her and Tad pick up their menus. She couldn't even fault the other customers in the diner who were staring at them, or the waitress who dropped a dish, or the woman who had walked past the table three times in one minute.

If she hadn't already seen Tad, she'd be just as frenzied as they were. Probably even more so. She'd probably run in and apply for a job and knock some other waitress out of the way in order to wait on Tad. Violence might be involved. She understood how everyone else felt. Getting this close to Tad was so exciting she could hardly stand it—

and she'd been there before; she'd even gotten to *kiss* him.

Tad studied the menu for a minute or two, then glanced up at her. "Okay, here's a question. What exactly is chicken-fried steak?"

Rosalee smiled. It was so weird to see Tad in her world, to be sitting at the diner instead of a fancy restaurant in L.A., to have him asking questions about the food this time. She had to admit—she liked it better this way.

"Is it chicken, or is it steak?" Tad asked. "I mean, I'm pretty confident it's fried, but…"

"It's steak. Fried like you fry a chicken," Rosalee explained.

"Then why not just call it fried steak?" Tad asked.

"Because no one would order that." Wasn't it obvious?

Tad scratched his head. "Then what's chicken-fried chicken?"

Rosalee laughed. "Are you going to question everything on the menu?"

"Just the real redundant stuff. Who makes the chicken-fried chicken—Chef the Cook?" Tad joked, and Rosalee laughed.

They closed their menus in synchronization and smiled at each other. Rosalee was so happy to see him again that it surprised her.

"So. Thanks for coming out with me," Tad said.

She gazed across the table at him. "I still can't

believe you're here."

Tad shrugged. "It was something I had to do."

"Fly clear across the country—and by the way, the social spectrum—to have lunch at the Fraziers Bottom Diner?" Rosalee asked.

But Tad wasn't joking around. "I couldn't let the other night be the last time I ever saw you," he explained.

"Okay, let me just stop you right there and remind you of one thing," Rosalee said.

"What's that?"

"You're Tad Hamilton. Do you understand?"

"So?" Tad didn't seem to get how strange this was.

"And I'm, you know, me," Rosalee reminded him.

"So? We're both human beings, aren't we?"

"No. I mean, yes. But I'm nobody," Rosalee insisted.

Tad looked at her as if she were crazy. "Nobody's nobody."

"Fine, but if anybody were nobody, it would be me." Rosalee tried not to analyze whether what she'd said made sense. She tended to talk in gibberish when Tad was nearby.

"I'm following my gut, Rosalee. Sometimes we have to do that, even if it seems crazy," Tad said. "Because in the gap between what prudence says we should do, and what our heart says we must do, well, therein lies our humanity."

Rosalee couldn't believe it. She burst out laughing.

"What?"

"That's from *The Road to El Dorado*." Did he really think she wouldn't remember, that she wouldn't recognize the lines? Didn't he know what a huge fan of his she was? "It's the speech you make right before you lead the daring nighttime escape past the entire Wyatt Earp clan."

"Oh." Tad looked a little embarrassed, but then he recovered with a smile. "You *are* a big fan, aren't you."

"That's what you do to get girls? You steal lines from your own movies?" Rosalee teased him.

"Not anymore," Tad muttered, hanging his head a little bit.

"I hope not," Rosalee said. "Don't be doing that. That shoots a serious hole in your credibility."

"Sorry." He grinned. "You gotta admit, though, I picked a good speech."

"It was a good speech—written by Sheldon Meltzner and David Crumm." He didn't seriously expect to get credit for someone else's words, did he?

"True. But I mean, I changed it around," Tad boasted. "It was weird their way."

"Mm-hm."

Tad sat up straighter on the vinyl bench seat. "Look, Rosalee. The truth is, when we went on our date, you said you were sure I had my priorities straight. But here's the thing. I don't," Tad confessed, shaking his head. "I really don't. And I want to get them straight. Because you were right—my life is unsatisfying. And so I need a positive influence. I need to be around a solid and substantial person who understands life and knows how to live it in a good and happy way. Like you. I just want to be around you, Rosalee. I just want a little bit of your goodness to rub off on me."

Did he come up with that on his own? Rosalee briefly wondered. Or was that from some forthcoming movie she hadn't yet seen?

Well, either way, she needed a little clarification before she jumped into this…whatever it was. "Can I ask you…would that be a romantic goodness, or a platonic goodness?" she said.

"A platonic goodness. And I mean that very seriously," Tad insisted. "No funny business here."

No funny business. Does that mean no more kisses? "Oh." Rosalee sighed.

Tad put his hand on her arm. "Did I say something wrong?" he asked, concerned.

"No, no, it's…uh…no." *Good cover, Rosalee. Very convincing.* "So does this mean you're going to stay in Fraziers Bottom for a while?"

"I have to. This is the ashram, and you're the guru," Tad said. "Besides, if I'm gonna change my life, I gotta get out of L.A. I gotta get out of the fishbowl."

Rosalee glanced at the people who were still staring at them through the big window. She knew what Tad meant, but they couldn't be more in a fishbowl than they were right now without having to swim. "Tad Hamilton wants my goodness to platonically rub off on him," she said, trying to absorb what he'd said. Something about an ashram and a guru.

"That's exactly correct," Tad said.

"Yikes a bee," Rosalee breathed.

Tad smiled. "I beg your pardon?"

"Oh, that's just a thing my Dad and I say sometimes, when life surprises you in that way that it has, and it doesn't matter anyway because there's no place to go but forward."

Tad nodded in appreciation. "See, I think I'm improving already."

Pete watched as Rosalee and Tad shook hands in the parking lot. *They're shaking hands, not kissing,* Pete observed. *That has to mean something. Things didn't work out—things aren't going to work out. He's leaving for the airport immediately.*

He watched as Rosalee turned away from Tad's rental car and made her way through the crowd of people around the store. Pete had been standing at the window waiting for her to come back practically ever since she left—of course, he kept coming up with excuses to be at the front of the store, so he didn't seem *that* obvious. When he saw her coming into the store, Pete ran off to check on something over by the customer service desk, so that she wouldn't see him.

The entire store started to applaud when she walked in. Everyone was whistling and clapping and cheering for Rosalee. It was disgusting. So she ate lunch with a major movie star. So what? Since when did people get applause for eating? He ate every day—several times, in fact. Did anyone cheer for him?

"He wants your goodness to rub off on him?" Pete scoffed, disgusted.

Rosalee had just emerged from the office, and told him about her lunch with Tad and what he'd said to her. She was going out with him again that night—to the movies, she said.

"That's right." Rosalee seemed almost proud about it.

"I see. And you…actually believe this?" Pete asked. He followed her up to her register.

"Why wouldn't I?" she questioned.

Pete shook his head in disbelief. "Rosalee, I just don't even know what to say. I mean, there's 'innocent,' there's 'childlike,' and then there's just 'asking for it.'"

"Pete—"

"Wants your goodness to rub off on him…" Pete repeated. He couldn't get over the nerve—and the phoniness—of this guy. What he wanted wasn't Rosalee's goodness. It was *her*. In every way. But Tad wasn't going to get near her, if Pete could help it. "Well, fortunately, you can't go to the movies with him tonight, anyway," he said.

Rosalee turned around and stared at him. "What do you mean, I can't?"

"I need you to stay on for the late shift," Pete lied. "Poor Janine, she's coughing like an old man in a Russian novel."

Rosalee glanced over at Janine, who was standing behind the register next to hers. "She is not."

"Janine, cough for me," Pete instructed her.

"Huh?" Janine replied.

"*Cough* for me, Janine." *Janine was a poor choice,* Pete thought as he walked over to her. She didn't catch on all that quickly—she never had.

Janine did a small, pathetic cough, sounding as if she were politely trying to interrupt someone—not sounding sick in the slightest.

"You hear that? It's all in her lungs." Pete nodded knowingly at Rosalee.

Janine clutched her hand to her chest, looking panicked. "What is?"

"Nothing, Janine, you're fine," Rosalee assured her.

"You're not fine," Pete said. He turned to Rosalee. "Kindly don't tell my employees when they're fine."

"She's fine," Rosalee insisted. "And even if she weren't, you'd have to find someone else to work that late shift, Petey. Because I am going out with Tad Hamilton!" Rosalee declared happily. She sounded a little angry with him, at the same time, and she stormed off to find Cathy, completely abandoning her post at register 5.

Pete went over to apologize to a lone customer, as he placed the "Lane Closed" sign on the conveyor belt.

Behind him, Janine coughed a few times, rather pathetically.

"Stop that!" Pete told her over his shoulder.

"I'm sorry, Mr. Hamilton, but there would be no point in moving you to another room," the desk clerk informed Tad, who'd phoned the desk from his room. If you could call it a room—closet was more like it, Tad thought. He might as well be sleeping in his car. He'd checked in a few minutes ago, but he had no idea exactly what he was signing up for.

"Every room is exactly the same," the desk clerk explained. "Every room in every Nationwide Inn in the whole nation is exactly the same. That's the whole point of Nationwide Inn."

"Do you have any suites?" Tad asked. If he didn't get more room in his…room, he was going to go crazy. Already he felt claustrophobic, and he'd only been in the room for five minutes.

"Suites? Well, we have some lollies down here by the register," the clerk said helpfully. He paused. Then, finally getting it, he went on. "Oh. I understand. No, we have no suites."

"Okay, that's cool," Tad said. Just then, his cell phone rang. "Hang on just one second," he told the clerk as he grabbed his cell phone from the bed, leaving the room phone lying beside him. "Hello?"

"Where are you?" Richard Levy, his agent, demanded.

"I'm in a motel in Fraziers Bottom, West Virginia," Tad said cheerfully. He knew this might come as a shock to the Richards, but they'd have to deal with it—they'd understand, once he explained.

"Okay. Words I have never heard anyone utter before," his agent said with a little disdain.

"She's special, Richard." Tad pictured Rosalee's face, how she'd looked when he walked into the Piggly Wiggly that afternoon and surprised her. She was such a natural beauty.

"Who?" Richard asked.

"The girl from the charity thing," Tad said.

"The Win-a-Date girl?"

Tad wished he wouldn't say it like that, as if Richard were already making her into a product he could sell. "Yes," he said.

"Let me understand this," his agent said. "You flew to a place actually called Fraziers Bottom, West Virginia, and are staying in a motel in order to nail the Win-a-Date girl?"

I should have known he wouldn't get it. "I don't want to 'nail' her. Please don't put it in those terms."

"Oh, forgive me, Lord Byron," Richard said sarcastically.

"I just want to be around her," Tad said.

"Uh-huh." His agent sounded as if he had never heard of such a concept.

"She has a goodness," Tad explained.

"Right…"

"There's a lot I can learn from her."

"Nail, nail, nail, you are trying to nail her!" Tad's agent cried. "And the sick thing is, you don't even realize that you're trying to nail her."

How could this Richard be so off the mark? His manager Richard—well, Tad would understand if *he* didn't get it. But he'd always imagined his agent had a tiny bit of a soul under those layers of chemically peeled skin. "Look, she was your idea," Tad reminded him. "You were the one who said wholesomeness would be good for me."

"Yes, image-wise," Richard agreed. "Not in real *life*."

"Well, you were righter than you knew," Tad said.

"No, I wasn't. I have never been righter than I knew."

"I'm trying to feed my soul, Richard, okay? I'm trying to find a way to actually be…happy." It sounded so strange when he said it out loud. Strange and a little trite. But it was the truth; that was what he wanted.

"Happy? You want to be happy now?" Richard sounded incredulous.

"Don't you want me to do something healthy?" Tad asked.

"'Happy' and 'healthy.' You sound like my Uncle George on New Year's Eve," Richard scoffed.

Of course Richard wouldn't understand, Tad thought. Richard, his agent, the most superficial, cynical, money-hungry man on the planet—besides Richard, his manager. "This is big for me, Richard. It's a turning point."

"That's what you think today. But by the end of the week, when you've nailed her, you're suddenly going to feel differently. And what do you suppose happens then?" Richard asked.

"I—"

"I will tell you what happens then," he interrupted. "You break—no, you pulverize—her heart. You smash it into tiny heart *granules.* And then the press finds out that you granulated the heart of the innocent small-town girl who thought she was so lucky because she won a date with you, and all the good that was done by the promotion gets washed away in an ocean of everybody's pain. And there's a humongous under-the-table cash settlement. And Jimmy Ing continues breathing. In fact, now he's taking big, deep diaphragmatic breaths, like an opera singer."

Tad sighed in frustration. "You're not listening to me, Richard."

"I am listening. I'm just trying not to hear. A

person like you cannot have a relationship with a girl from Montana."

"West Virginia," Tad corrected him. "And why not?"

"You're too different!" Richard stated. "Your values are different. For example, she has them."

That was a low blow, Tad thought. Sure, he'd been a bit naughty at times, but he wasn't completely devoid of values. Some of them, anyway. "It can work," Tad insisted to Richard, for what felt like the hundredth time. This was a good decision. So why was he spending so much time defending it to someone who didn't get it?

"It can't," Richard said. "And when it ends, it'll be very bad for business."

"There are more important things than business!" Tad argued.

There was a silence on the other end of the phone, and then Richard said, "I don't even know who I'm talking to now."

Tad decided he was done with this conversation. It was pointless. He'd been having the best day of his life, and his agent's call was ruining it for him. "I gotta go," he said quickly.

"No, you don't. You do not gotta go," Richard shot back. "What you gotta do is understand that you're going through some kind of a phase right now, some kind of a phase thing, some kind of an extreme version of your normal in-between-jobs insanity, and it has a hold of you, and I do not at the moment have a job for you that will break that hold, which means you must break that hold yourself, by other means. You need to come back to L.A., go out on a date with an actress looking to advance her career, and put an end to all this self-destructive behavior!"

No deal, Tad thought. He was staying right where he was. "I'll see you soon, okay?" he said, pulling his cell phone away from his ear, about to hang up.

"No! No, Tad—" He heard Richard's voice still talking.

"Good-bye, Richard," he said calmly.

"Fine! Fine. Your career, the sane portion of you, and I will look forward to your call!"

There was a loud crash on Richard's end of the line just as Tad switched off the phone. He shrugged and took some deep breaths, calling on the meditation yoga he'd learned for a part once. Let Richard get all riled up and upset. He wasn't going to let Richard talk him out of this, the best idea he'd had in years.

Suddenly Tad realized he had left the hotel phone lying on the bed beside him, off the hook. "Hello?" he said into the receiver.

"Yes, Mr. Hamilton, I am here," the clerk replied politely.

"Oh, good, thank you."

"Thought I lost you there. I was willing to invest a little more time, though," the desk clerk said. "I figured if you needed to keep me on hold, that was okay by me—on hold would I be for you, sir."

"Um…you wouldn't have a masseuse on staff, would you?" Tad asked, rubbing his shoulder. This tension from the phone call had traveled straight to his neck and shoulders.

"A what?" the clerk asked.

Tad sighed, hung up the phone, and lay down on the bed, resting his head on a couple of ridiculously flat pillows stacked together. What was he worried about, anyway? He didn't need a massage.

He needed Rosalee. Seeing Rosalee tonight would get rid of all the tension he was feeling right now.

CHAPTER NINE

I hope this is good enough. Rosalee examined her reflection in the full-length mirror on the back of her bedroom door. She was wearing jeans and a sweater—very casual. They were going out for a casual evening—this wasn't like going to one of the best restaurants in L.A.—or even to one of the best in Fraziers Bottom.

She fixed her hair one last time, then walked down to the living room, where Tad was having a drink with her father. "Hi," she greeted Tad, smiling.

"Hi!" Tad's face lit up when she walked into the room.

"I see you've met Dad," she commented.

"Yeah—we've been talking shop," Tad said, and her father looked pleased with himself.

"So, what should we do tonight?" Rosalee asked.

"Well, do you guys have a movie theater?" Tad asked.

"The Rialto," Rosalee said with a smile. It was where she'd seen all of Tad's movies. Repeatedly.

"It's part of the Loews Family of Theaters," her father said, trying to impress Tad with his knowledge of the film business. He'd been studying entertainment-industry Web sites all afternoon, ever since she told him that Tad would be coming over to pick her up that night.

"Have you seen *King Arthur of Britain*?" Rosalee asked Tad.

"Been wanting to," he replied.

Rosalee wasn't sure whether he was telling the truth or not. But in the end, who cared?

"It's an armor-plated jouster that should crusade to solid ducat," Mr. Futch said.

Rosalee thought her father was laying it on a little thick. "We could get a bite, after," she suggested to Tad.

He grinned, as if he were looking forward to the evening. "God bless you, Rosalee," he said as they headed for the front door.

"Well, you two enjoy yourselves. Have her back by four A.M.," Mr. Futch said to Tad.

"How was I?" her father whispered out of the corner of his mouth as Rosalee walked past him.

"You were great, Daddy," Rosalee said as she breezed past him.

Pete pressed the remote button as he sat on his couch. A movie about World War I was on—starring Tad Hamilton. Rosalee would know the title of it, but Pete didn't and he was proud of that fact. Tad was running across a war zone and miraculously not getting blown to bits by the mortar shells exploding all around him.

He sighed and changed channels to get away from Tad's heroic image, which he'd seen too much of lately. He landed on a talk show where Tad was being interviewed. Again, not what he wanted to see.

What was wrong with cable TV, he wondered. Didn't the channels coordinate with each other, at all? Was there no such thing as a Tad Hamilton–free zone?

Beside Pete, his dog, Rochelle, looked up at him with a slightly concerned expression.

Pete patted her head and switched to the next channel. It was Telemundo, and Tad was pitching a soft drink, smiling at the camera and saying, *"Hasta el próximo miércoles!"*

Pete lifted the remote to his head, pressed it against his skull, and pushed the channel button.

"So, what do people do at this point in the evening in Fraziers Bottom, West Virginia?" Tad asked as he held the car door open for Rosalee.

They'd both really enjoyed the movie, although for a while Rosalee couldn't get used to the fact that Tad Hamilton the person was sitting in the theater where she always went to see Tad Hamilton the actor. People kept elbowing each other and pointing him out and giggling. Even weirder was walking past the life-sized Tad cardboard cutout advertising his next movie, *The Secret Life of Thieves.*

Tad got into the car and looked over at Rosalee for an answer.

"Well, they go to the diner. . . ." Rosalee suggested.

"We could do that," Tad agreed. "We haven't eaten anything in almost fifteen minutes."

Rosalee laughed. "Or they go home. . . ." she said slowly. Not that she really wanted to do that.

"It is a school night," Tad said.

Then another idea occurred to Rosalee. She wasn't sure it was a good one, but it definitely was an idea. "Of course, if it were a date, we might go to the Water Gap Overlook," she said.

"What do people do there?" Tad asked.

"They...park."

"And then?" Tad paused, his hand on the car key, not yet turning the ignition.

"Well, they marvel at what a feat of engineering the gap is," Rosalee explained. "Representing, as it does, the indomitable spirit of the West Virginian."

Tad nodded, grinning. "Really."

"Mm-hm." Rosalee pictured the scene: the two of them sitting in the car at Water Gap Overlook, holding hands, then kissing. . . .

"No. We can't do that," Tad suddenly said.

"We can't?" Rosalee felt her heart sink.

"No. Not that I don't want to!" Tad held up his hands. "Because I do. I really want to. But I won't do anything that might harm the friendship," he said.

Rosalee knew what he was saying made sense. Normally she could go along with that a hundred percent. But tonight? When she and Tad were having such a good time together, and she was so attracted to him? But she had to trust him. "I won't, either," she declared, feeling very proud of herself for being so strong.

"I mean, I really, really want to. But I won't. I'm here for a reason. I can't lose sight of that," Tad said. "This is the ashram, you are the guru. This is the ashram, you are the guru," he repeated. "This is the—"

"Okay," Rosalee interrupted him. She wasn't sure she wanted to be a guru, if it meant passing up going to Water Gap Overlook with Tad.

He looked away from her. "We gotta just simmer down and stay with the program."

"You're right," Rosalee agreed, turning to face forward in her seat, keeping as much distance between them as possible so she wouldn't feel so tempted.

"I should take you home," Tad said.

"You should?"

"Yes." Tad nodded. "Because home is…where

89

the heart is…and there's no place like it…and it's sweet," he babbled.

"So…we're calling it a night?" Rosalee asked.

"That's right," Tad agreed. "This night is over."

Rosalee let out a tiny sigh as they pulled out of the Rialto Theater's parking lot.

"Over two trillion gallons of water…" Rosalee whispered into Tad's ear between kisses. "Flow through the Gap…" she murmured, before Tad kissed her again. "Every hour," Rosalee said breathlessly.

"Mm." Tad could not stop kissing her, and he had a feeling he was never going to hear the end of the story. It was so cute of her to keep trying to tell him about it. It made him want to kiss her even more.

They'd tried to go home, go their separate ways, call it a night. They really had. But then Rosalee had started talking about how he should really see this place, and then he'd asked her to show it to him, and then…well.

"That's enough water…to float a battleship…or put out every fire in West Virginia…for four and a half years," Rosalee said, getting in a few words between each kiss.

Suddenly, as if from a great distance, Tad heard a ringing noise. It took him a few seconds to realize that it was his cell phone.

"Uh-oh," Rosalee said.

"Excuse me." Tad regretfully pulled away from Rosalee to pick up the phone. He started to look at the Caller ID, but then thought better of it. What was he doing, answering his phone now? He didn't care who was calling. He didn't care if he ever got a call on his cell phone again.

He opened the car window and threw the phone out over the edge of the scenic overlook. Then he turned back to Rosalee and smiled. "Come here," he said softly.

Don't do it, Pete said to himself as he drummed his fingers against the arms of the sofa. *Just don't. Restrain yourself. Only someone desperate would do something like that.*

He grabbed the phone and hit the prepro-grammed speed-dial button.

"Hello?" Mr. Futch answered a few seconds later.

"Hi, Mr. Futch, it's Pete." He tried to sound casual.

"Hiya, Pete. Rosie's not here," Mr. Futch said. "She's out with Tad Hamilton." He seemed very proud about that fact, which made Pete think that Rosalee's dad had no idea about Tad's semi-checkered past.

But Pete decided to play dumb. That way, maybe he wouldn't seem like he was checking up on her, even though that was exactly what he was trying to do. "Oh, is that right? Wow—good for her, huh?" he said cheerfully. This was killing him. *Killing* him.

"He seems like a very nice guy," Mr. Futch remarked.

"He does. A lovely, lovely guy," Pete said with a hint of sarcasm. "So, where did they go?"

"The movies."

Pete grabbed the newspaper from the floor and opened it to the movie section to look at times. "The movies. How nice, how subtly self-aggrandizing." He checked out the Rialto's ad. "Okay. Well, looks like the seven o'clock show breaks at about eight forty-five or eight fifty. Or, so I think someone happened to mention to me. Very much in passing." He coughed nervously as he looked up at the clock. "So that would put them, uh, out and about already, and onto their next activity."

"I guess it would, Pete." Mr. Hutch didn't seem the slightest bit concerned about it. "I'll leave Rosie a note that you called."

"Yeah, I, uh, I just had a little inventory question," Pete said to cover for the fact he was fishing for information. "A little dairy case inventory, uh, query. But we'll clear that up, you know, whenever."

Pete hung up the phone and stared at the wall for a second. Where did people go after the movies, when they wanted to be alone? It wasn't that hard to figure out. He grabbed his car keys and headed for the door.

Please don't be there. That was all Pete could think as he headed up the hill above town. *Just don't.* Maybe they were at the diner, or maybe Tad's hotel room.

Wait. How would that be better? Pete shook his head. He told himself that he knew Rosalee was a better person than that. She didn't just go out with anyone. For instance…him. She didn't go out with him. But that was okay, he respected her for that. Besides, it wasn't as if he'd asked her out, yet, or ever. He was working up to that. Some guys, like Tad, took only minutes. Pete took years.

He pulled into the parking lot at the Water Gap Overlook. Oh, no. There they were—Pete cruised closer to get a better look—sitting in Tad's infamous rental car.

Actually, they weren't just sitting. They were all over each other. They didn't even notice him go by, because they were too busy making out. In fact, Pete was surprised that they *hadn't* just gone to Tad's motel room—they might as well have. They'd be sparing innocent people such as himself from seeing this.

But they hadn't, had they? They were subjecting him and everyone else to this…this…disgusting display. So maybe they should pay for that little mistake.

"The hydroelectric plant at Raintree…generates enough energy each week…to run a string of seventy-five-watt light bulbs…from here to Gallup, New Mexico," Rosalee said as she and Tad kept kissing. They hadn't stopped since the moment they'd parked here. Normally Rosalee wouldn't act like this, but being with Tad Hamilton wasn't normal.

"Rosalee?" Tad said, pushing a strand of hair off her face.

"Yes?" she asked breathlessly.

"I really, really like my guru," Tad said. He leaned in for another kiss.

Suddenly someone knocked on the driver's side window, and they both jumped.

Tad turned the ignition key partway to lower the automatic window, smoothing his hair down a bit as he did. Rosalee tried to compose herself as a blue police uniform came into view.

The policeman leaned slightly into the car. "May I see your license and registration—" He stared at Tad, and his expression changed from a frown to a smile. "Jesus Christ!"

Tad smiled right back at him. "Hello, officer."

The police officer looked over at Rosalee, and she wanted to sink under the seat. "Rosalee?" he asked, sounding stunned.

"Hi, Tom," she said, embarrassed.

"Jesus Christ," Officer Tom said again. He appeared to be in shock.

Hadn't Tom ever seen people making out at Water Gap Overlook before? Rosalee thought. *It was no big deal.* "Okay then," she said, wondering if they could move on now.

"We heard you were in town, Mr. Hamilton," the police officer said.

"Did you?" Tad asked.

"Fond of our Rosalee, huh?" Tom asked.

"Uh, yes, officer."

"Tom?" *Can we go now?* Rosalee felt like screaming. Can we get out of this incredibly embarrassing situation any time soon?

"Forgive me for bothering you," Tom went on. "We got a call saying someone was parked. It's illegal after sunset."

"You got a call at this hour? From who, a raccoon?" Rosalee asked.

But just as she asked, she heard a loud, roaring car engine. The kind of engine that didn't quite work right. The kind of engine that was missing a few key exhaust parts. *Pete's Mustang engine,* she thought as she craned her neck to see his car pulling out of the parking lot.

"Never mind," Rosalee said to Tom.

"Say, listen, I hate to ask, but could I impose for a very fast autograph for my daughter?" Tom wanted to know. "She would just be thrilled."

"I am going to tear Pete's head off and feed it to him on a big chicken stick!" Rosalee fumed.

She and Tad were standing outside her house, saying good night. Rosalee was so mad that she could hardly talk right. Why did Pete have to bust them like that? And embarrass her in front of one of the very few police officers in town who she was going to see every day for the rest of her life.

"Okay, okay, calm down," Tad said, putting his arm around her shoulders. "Because it doesn't matter. What happened tonight was a force of nature. Two people set out to be friends, but nature would have none of it. Nature wanted them to be more," Tad reasoned. "And nature is still going to want that tomorrow. That's how nature is. We've been pulled toward each other, Rosalee, by the gravity of the universe. We've crossed a line. We've *evolved*. And there's no going back."

Rosalee looked over at him, at his eyes shining with excitement, or maybe it was actually the streetlights reflecting off his eyes, but she didn't care. "You speak very well," she told him.

"Thank you."

They turned toward each other and stared into each other's eyes, leaning into each other, holding hands. "You gonna be all right 'til lunch tomorrow?" Rosalee asked. *Because I'm not sure if I am.*

"Oh yes. I'm going to check out some of Fraziers Bottom's top tourist spots," Tad said.

"Such as?" Rosalee asked.

"Such as the Museum of Sewing. Located right here in town."

Rosalee patted his arm. "We'll make it an early lunch."

"Good idea," Tad agreed.

Rosalee kissed him good night and then headed

up the sidewalk to her house. Before going inside, she turned around to wave at him. Tad tapped his mouth with three fingers and then gestured toward her, blowing her a kiss.

Rosalee felt like she was floating on air as she walked through the door.

CHAPTER **TEN**

"*What* did I tell you? What did I tell you about your feet?" Pete demanded.

Rosalee kept scanning the items coming toward her on the conveyor belt. She had a long line of customers, but did Pete jump in and open another register? No. He was too busy yelling at her, revealing private details about her. He was definitely not going to win Manager of the Year from her. In fact he could think about returning some of those precious plaques any time now.

"You said, keep one on the floor," she said to Pete.

"I said keep one on the floor. And did you? No!" Pete cried.

"You make it sound like some sleazy night!" Rosalee punched in the code for zucchini. "But it wasn't. It was classy."

"Right. It's not like you went to the movies and then made out in his car," Pete said dryly.

Why was she going over all of this with him? She didn't owe him an explanation. "The evening evolved, Pete," she said.

"Is that what he said?" Pete scoffed.

Technically yes, Rosalee thought, *but I agreed; that was exactly what happened.* "It started as two friends going to the movies," she explained.

"And it evolved into kissy face," Pete finished, sounding very critical.

"He fought it!" Rosalee said, not that Pete deserved to know everything. "He didn't want to do anything that might harm the friendship."

"Oh, God, he actually used that line?" Pete laughed loudly, beginning to sound a little hysterical. "And you actually bought it?"

Rosalee stopped scanning and glared at him. "It's not a '*line.*'"

Pete leaned forward to get the attention of everyone in line waiting to check out at Rosalee's register. "Okay, guys, show of hands. Who here has ever used some form of the 'I don't want to do anything that might harm the friendship' line?" he asked.

Rosalee didn't care what Pete said. The way Tad had said it, it wasn't a line, she thought angrily as every guy standing in front of her raised his hand. Her eyes widened as she saw even the Episcopal minister in town raise his hand. "Father Newell?"

she exclaimed in disbelief.

"Well, it was prior to my enfrockment," Father Newell replied calmly.

Rosalee cleared her throat. She had to explain to everyone. "Tad and I are beginning a profound, lasting relationship," she said.

"He is not *capable* of a profound, lasting relationship," Pete argued.

"What are you basing that on, the tabloids?" Rosalee asked. "You don't even read the tabloids. You read *Modern Grocer*."

"You don't have to read the tabloids to know about this guy. Martians know about this guy," Pete retorted.

Rosalee wasn't going to let him trash Tad anymore. Maybe Tad had made some mistakes in the past—big mistakes. But he was trying to become a better person, and she was going to help him do that. "He's turning over a new leaf," she said as she resumed scanning items.

"He's not, Rosie, and even if he were, that's all the more reason to wait before you go any further with him," Pete said.

Rosalee could not believe Pete wouldn't shut up about this. Wasn't he embarrassed? Because she certainly was. "Oh, Petey, good Lord," she said.

"What would be the most common progression, fellas?" Pete called out to the guys in line. "The 'I don't want to do anything to harm the friendship' line, followed by a more intense relationship, followed by…all together now…"

"It's not you, it's me," everyone chanted loudly in unison.

"Thank you," Pete told the group. He turned back to Rosalee. "After which, by the way, the friendship is generally harmed."

"Stop it, the bunch of you!" Rosalee called to the crowd. "Father Newell, stop giggling—you're just embarrassing yourself, now. Look," she said to Pete. "The normal rules don't apply to this situation."

Pete rolled his eyes. "Every person who ever got their heart broken has said that to themselves at one time or another."

Rosalee felt like she was wasting her breath. "You know, I really shouldn't be surprised that you're saying all this. You've only criticized every single thing I've ever done in my life."

Pete looked sort of hurt when she said that. "I'm just looking out for you, Rosie," he pleaded. "I'm just a cop on the Emotional Police Force, just walking my beat."

"Well, go to a donut shop. Get off duty," Rosie said. "I can take care of myself."

"Hey, Rosie. What are Tad's pectorals like, to the touch?" Cathy called from the next register. "Are they warm yet firm, like buttery leather over gun metal?"

"That's not helping," Pete said, exasperated.

"Sorry. Got caught up," Cathy apologized.

"Tad Hamilton is an *actor,* Rosie. Ever think he might be acting with you?" Pete asked.

"He's not acting," she insisted. Maybe Pete couldn't see that, because he didn't know Tad yet, but she could.

Pete came closer to her, gently turning her away from the price scanner. "He's playing a role. Maybe he doesn't realize it—I'm willing to give him that. But he's playing a role just the same—the role of the bad boy trying to find virtue. And soon, you know what he'll be doing?"

"What?" Rosalee asked.

"Moving on to his next role," Pete said.

Rosalee turned away from him and went back to work.

"I'm gonna make another prediction, all right?" Pete went on, sounding overly convinced that he was psychic all of a sudden. "After he's been with you for a while, that guy is *out of here. Gone. You will never see him again.*"

Before she could hit him, because that was practically the most insulting thing anyone had ever said to her, least of all one of her supposed best friends, Rosalee heard the automatic doors whir open.

Tad ran into the grocery store, jumping up and down, pumping his fists in the air. "I bought a house! I bought a house!" he cried.

Rosalee nearly dropped the jar of spaghetti

sauce in her hand.

"Actually a farm. I bought a farm! With a house! And a silo! For my wheat!" He threw his arms around Rosalee, hugging her. Then he picked her up and twirled her around in celebration.

"Really?" She looked over Tad's shoulder at Pete. "You bought a house?"

"We're putting down roots, baby!" Tad said. "I mean, you already have roots, but I'm putting down roots. Near your roots. So that our two root systems can become all entwined. How would that be?"

Rosalee smiled at him. "Good. That would be good."

"Come see it. Come see my house and my farm and my wheat."

"I'd love to!" Rosalee said.

Pete came closer to them, and Rosalee waited for him to say that she couldn't go now, because she had to wait until after her shift, and that her shift would last the next ten years.

Instead he surprised her, "Me, too. I'd absolutely love to."

Rosalee glared at Pete, while Tad looked a bit uncomfortable. "Uh…great," he said to Pete.

"Definitely!" Cathy called over from her register.

"You realize this means nothing," Pete said.

He was driving Rosalee and Cathy down a dirt

road on the outskirts of Fraziers Bottom. His old Mustang was rattling with each and every rut in the road. If parts fell off because of this trip, he was suing Tad Hamilton. Or, Tad could make things easy on himself, and simply buy Pete a new car.

"You are unbelievable," Rosalee said as she gazed out the window.

"These people buy houses all the time, Rosie. They don't care. It's like a tax shelter or something." The car hit a bump and Pete struggled to hold onto the steering wheel.

"You are just the most pathetic person I have ever been in a very old car with," Rosalee said.

Me? Pathetic? I'm not the one convinced some Hollywood star actually cares about me. "Rosalee, I will personally guarantee you that by the end of the day, Tad's farm and his house and his friggin' wheat will be back on the market," Pete said.

Rosalee looked suspicious. "Why? What are you going to do?"

"Nothing! Just be a good neighbor," Pete said. In truth he wasn't sure exactly what he was going to do, but he would think of something. You didn't get to be Manager of the Month for so many consecutive months without being able to think on your feet.

"I don't like the sound of that," Rosalee said warily.

"Just don't worry." Pete glanced over at her. "By the way, you haven't said anything about the shoulder harness."

"I'm sorry?"

"Well, they didn't make shoulder harnesses on this model Mustang. But I just had them added, because sometimes I carry some important cargo," Pete said. He looked over at her again just before they went over a bridge and the road narrowed slightly. "And you haven't said anything."

Rosalee pulled on the seat belt. "It's good. It's a very good shoulder harness."

Pete smiled. "I'm glad you like it."

"I don't see any shoulder harnesses in the back seat," Cathy complained.

They came to the top of a hill and there it was—the house Tad had described. Rosalee and Cathy shrieked in admiration as the Mustang pulled into the long, circular drive. The house sat on a huge piece of property, with tall, old trees, beautiful wildflowers, and a large gray barn and a blue silo behind it. The view from the top of the hill, when he got out of the car, was majestic, tremendous. *Sickening, even*, Pete thought. He felt like he was about to explode, or was it implode? It was hard to remember the exact word he was looking for when he was feeling so sick with envy.

Tad must have heard them drive up, because he

walked out onto the porch, a cowboy hat perched on his head.

"Howdy!" Tad called to the three of them.

Pete rolled his eyes, unable to hide his feelings. Since when was Tad Hamilton anything even remotely close to a cowboy?

"Tad, this is unbelievable!" Rosalee cried as she stepped up onto the porch.

"Thanks, little lady." Tad opened the screen door and gestured for them to go inside the house. "Why don't y'all come in and set a spell?"

"Ooookay," Pete said slowly.

Rosalee jabbed him in the ribs.

"Well, what is he, Reba McEntire suddenly?" Pete asked. Could the guy do nothing *but* act like other people? Did he have an original bone in his *GQ*-featured body?

Tad showed them around the house, which Pete had to admit was both gigantic and impressive— Rosalee and Cathy *ooh*ed and *aah*ed so much that he was afraid they were going to hyperventilate at some point. And then Tad led the three of them outside to the barn. "And these are what they call the south forty." Tad gestured to the land behind the house. "I'm not sure exactly how many acres it is, but…"

"I'm gonna guess forty," Pete said.

"Oh, right. Of course." Tad shook his head and laughed.

"So, Tad, listen." Pete moved a little closer to him, resting his elbows on the wooden fence. "If you want, I'd be happy to take you through some of the new tasks you'll be facing as a farm owner."

He noticed Rosalee cast a curious glance at him, but he ignored her. So he didn't currently own a farm—that was a minor detail.

"Would you?" Tad asked. "I'd really appreciate that."

"I mean, I'm sure you'll hire people to run the place, but still. I bet a guy like you wouldn't feel right owning a farm if he couldn't do the chores, right?" Pete asked.

Tad clapped him on the shoulder. "You're absolutely right, Pete."

Now things were going to get interesting, Pete thought. Once he showed Rosalee what an out-and-out fake Tad was, she'd completely lose interest in him.

About ten minutes later, Rosalee and Cathy were watching Pete and Tad prepare to milk a cow. Rosalee was doing her best to keep from heckling them both—but especially Pete. Since when had he ever milked a cow?

"Well, milk, Tad, huh?" Pete was saying, sounding very self-important. "The lifeblood of society. Now what you want to do is grab this thing, here, which is actually a nipple, and pull it firmly toward the pail," he instructed slowly, as if Tad needed extra time. "It's going to feel a little freaky the first time you—"

Pete stopped at the sound of milk hissing into a pail. Cathy and Rosalee looked at each other and cracked up laughing.

"Attagirl, Arlene," Tad said to the cow. "Attagirl. Nothing to it, baby. Nothing to it." He glanced over at Pete. "Remember my remake of *The Grapes of Wrath*?"

Pete nodded glumly.

After the cow-milking exhibition, they all moved to an open field behind the barn. Rosalee stood in the clearing, watching Tad and Pete gather wood they planned to split for firewood. She and Cathy had agreed that they didn't know what Pete was up to. Maybe he was genuinely trying to be a nice guy and give Tad some help getting settled in Fraziers Bottom. But then why did it seem like he was trying to prove something?

"Okay, so, the key is taking a full swing, so as to split the wood in one stroke." Pete positioned a log on the wide stump and lifted the ax over his shoulder. He took a strong swing at the log, but the ax only went halfway down. He angled the ax back and forth to pull it out of the log and try again. "Of course, sometimes, no matter what you do—"

Before he could take another swing at the log, Tad swung his ax, and with a loud "pop" split the log in one fell swoop. He picked up another log and split that one, too. Rosalee watched him, admiring his strength, while Pete kept hacking away at that first log, which he'd shaved into several small pieces.

"Pete, did you ever see a movie I did called *A Man Named Jackson*?" Tad asked, wiping sweat off his forehead with the sleeve of his shirt.

Rosalee smiled, thinking of Tad's role in that movie.

"If it came out, Tad, then I saw it," Pete said, standing back from the log and glaring at it as if he wanted to throw it back into the woods.

It was no surprise to Rosalee that when they got horses from the stables, Pete was at a disadvantage yet again. Pete went sprinting past Rosalee, on a horse that was obviously too fast for him.

"It's crucial that the horse knows who's in charge!" he called over his shoulder to Tad. "He needs to sense your strength and confidence!"

A few seconds later, Tad came stampeding out behind him, easily passing Pete. He whooped with excitement, guiding the horse's reins with one hand while he waved his cowboy hat in the air with the other. He looked so happy, and so natural, on the horse that it made Rosalee smile to watch him ride like that.

"The Life and Times of Whirlaway!" Tad called out as he galloped past Pete.

Right, Rosalee thought. *Of course! One of her favorite movies of all time.*

CHAPTER **ELEVEN**

The next night, Rosalee and Tad were standing by the bar in Li'l Dickens with Cathy, and assorted hangers-on, while Pete tried to distract himself by playing darts. It wasn't working all that well. He kept stopping to listen to Tad, getting mad at himself for doing that, and then his concentration was shot and he'd mis-throw all of his tosses.

Tad Hamilton needed to leave town immediately, in Pete's opinion. But it didn't look like that was going to happen.

"And how do you cry on command like you do?" Cathy was asking Tad.

"Me? I don't cry," Tad said. "I haven't cried since I was fourteen and I broke my femur."

"Don't tell me you don't cry," Cathy said. "You cried in *Return to Daktari*. You cried in *Three on the March*."

"No, I didn't. I *teared*," Tad corrected her.

Cathy's eyebrows creased. "What are you talking about?"

"I'll show you." Tad took a pack of cigarettes out of his shirt pocket. He shook one out of the pack, put it in his mouth, and then quickly lit it. "What you do is, you hold the cigarette at an angle so that the smoke gets in your eyes. You force yourself not to blink…and before too long…"

Tears welled in his eyes, and everyone in the crowd gathered around him, *ooh*ing and *ahh*ing. Everyone but Pete.

"Of course, you do it too much, you get retinal cancer," Tad joked. "Which is why I stay away from melodramas."

Everyone laughed, including Rosalee, who was standing so close to Tad that you'd think they were permanently attached.

"Is it weird when you have to French-kiss somebody you don't know?" Cathy asked him next.

"Well, depends on who it is," Tad answered. "If it's a gorgeous actress, that's cool. If it's some hot young male actor, that does get into kind of a weird area." Everyone started to laugh again. "But of course the truth is, you don't actually French-kiss them."

"You don't?" Cathy looked vaguely disappointed.

"No, no. See, on the screen it just looks like a French kiss. What you do is, you open your mouth and you move your jaw, but you don't actually use your tongue."

"Come on," Rosalee scoffed.

"Watch this." Tad leaned forward and kissed Rosalee, making it look as if he were French-kissing her. In Pete's opinion, one was almost as bad as the other. He could have done without the explanation—and especially without the demonstration.

"How'd that look?" Tad asked the group when he and Rosalee finally separated from each other's faces.

Horrible, Pete thought. *Disgusting.*

"Good. That looked good," Cathy said enviously, staring dreamily at Tad, and everyone around her laughed.

Rosalee playfully shoved Tad away from her. "I want you to kiss me for real, now."

"I think I can do that," Tad said with a grin. "Stand back, everybody."

No problem, Pete thought as he looked away from them and fired a quick throw at the dart board. The dart landed right in the bull's-eye. He fired another, and it too landed right in the center of the board, in the tiny red area. He aimed the third dart carefully and tossed. Yes! Triple bull's-eye!

"Wow! Wow! I did it! Hey, do you see this?" Pete cried. "Do you people see this? Rosalee?"

But when he turned around, he saw that no one had seen it—definitely not Rosalee. Her lips were still locked on Tad's, and the rest of the bar crowd was standing there, entranced, watching them.

"I'm just gonna…go to the men's room," Pete said to nobody in particular. "Excuse me."

Pete was just finishing up in the bathroom when Tad walked in, right past him, and opened a stall door. Before he could close the door, Pete hurried over and pulled it open. "Hi, Tad," he said.

"Hi, Pete."

"May I speak with you for a minute?" Pete asked. He wasn't sure what he was doing—yet. But he had to say something and he had a feeling this was the only chance he'd get to be alone with Tad. Even if it was under very strange circumstances.

Tad sat down on the closed toilet seat and glanced at him. "Uh, sure."

"Forgive the intrusion, but my courage is up, so…"

Tad held up his hands. "No, no. Please. Fire away."

"Okay." Pete took a deep breath to prepare himself. "I want to say that…you won. Rosalee's heart. You won it fair and square."

"Thanks, Pete." Tad sounded genuinely grateful for the acknowledgment.

"I mean, you did have some small advantages going in. Couple of hundred million dollars, the most recognizable face on five continents…" Pete paused. He could go on and on, about genetically perfect cheekbones and animal magnetism, but what point would there be? "But hey—you won. And I have to respect that. Congratulations."

"Thank you," Tad said again.

The men's room door opened and another customer walked in. He stopped when he saw Tad sitting on the toilet with the door open and Pete leaning against the door, talking to him.

"Do you mind? We're talking in here," Pete snapped at him.

The guy stared at them for another second before walking back out.

"Tad, I want you and Rosalee to be happy together," Pete continued. "If you're going to be with her, then I want you to be the right guy for her."

"That's very gracious," Tad commented.

"So I need to ask you, Tad. Do you know how long she keeps her hair in straight mode, and how long in curly?" Pete asked.

Tad looked confused. He definitely hadn't been expecting a quiz when he came into the men's room. "Um…what?" he asked.

"Do you know why her favorite necklace has a starfish clasp? Or how, on Sunday mornings, she reads the newspaper standing up, with the paper on the table, dancing a little as she turns the pages?" Pete asked.

"Uh, no?" Tad replied.

He was failing, miserably, Pete thought. "Do you

know…how many smiles she has?"

Tad wrinkled his nose. "How many smiles?"

"She has six." Pete thought about it, reviewing his mental inventory. He'd noticed this over the years. He'd never made it this official, or written it down or anything. It was just something he knew, and he wanted the guy whom she was falling for to know about them, too.

"One when something really makes her laugh," Pete began. "One when she's just laughing out of politeness. One when she makes plans. One when she makes fun of herself. One when she's uncomfortable. And one when she's talking about her friends."

Tad didn't respond for a minute. "I don't know those things yet, Pete," he finally admitted.

"No, you don't. Which is my point. Tad, as much as you may love her, she is more of a treasure than you can possibly imagine." Pete knew he was going on a bit of a tirade, but he felt like it was deserved. "She's not just some good-hearted, healthy-for-you, wholesome, small-town girl— some breath of fresh air. She's an amazing person with a huge heart and the kind of beauty a man only sees once in his lifetime. She's the woman you compare every other woman to, but they never measure up. She's the one," Pete declared. "So if there's even a chance that you might wind up breaking her heart, I want you to leave her be, Tad. To leave her be and get out of Fraziers Bottom."

Pete stopped, sort of amazed by himself. He didn't think he'd ever given such a long speech before.

Tad nodded and smiled up at him. "I could never hurt Rosalee, Pete. The old Tad could have. But she's taught this Tad a few things. This Tad knows better."

Pete looked at his expression, trying to gauge whether he was being honest with him or not. This was the man who had just taught people how to fake crying and how to fake a good kiss. How much was he faking here?

"I want to believe you," Pete said. "And I believe that *you* believe you, which makes you very winning and charming in a potentially hugely dangerous sort of way."

"You can believe me," Tad insisted. "I'll never break her heart."

"Good. Because if you do, I'm going to tear you to pieces with my bare hands." Pete thought about that for a moment. "Or my vicious rhetoric," he added.

Tad looked up at him. "You're a good guy, Pete."

"Thanks. Not, um, apparently not good enough, though," he muttered.

"Could I, uh…?" Tad cleared his throat.

"Sorry, yes, sure." Pete backed away from the bathroom stall and walked back out into the bar. He didn't know what he'd been trying to accomplish, exactly—he just felt like he needed to stick up for Rosalee and protect her. Just in case things didn't work out the way she wanted them to.

He saw her sitting at the bar with Cathy, and she looked back at him expectantly, as if she were hoping he was Tad. When she saw it was just Pete, her face fell a little. He waved at her and went over to sit with some friends from work.

"You're a good kisser," Rosalee said to Tad. They had just gotten back to his room at the Nationwide Inn from Li'l Dickens. Naturally, they'd gone straight to their favorite activity. "But then I'm guessing it doesn't come as a shock to you to hear that."

"You're a really good kisser," Tad replied as he nuzzled Rosalee's neck.

"I am?" she asked.

"Mm-hmm."

"Even compared to Hollywood girls?"

"Mm-hmm."

"Well," Rosalee said, thinking about it for a second. "That's just ridiculous." She leaned against Tad, and he ran his hands down her arms, making her shiver. Then he pulled her even closer for a passionate kiss.

There was a knock at the door, and Rosalee flinched. *Not Officer Tom again,* she thought. *There's nothing illegal going on here. Why can't everyone just leave us alone?*

"Tad?" a man's voice called out. There was

another knock on the door.

"Are you in there, pal?" a different voice asked.

Tad grumbled and clenched his hair with his hands. "You gotta be kidding me!" he said, sounding exasperated.

CHAPTER **TWELVE**

"Who are they?" Rosalee asked.

"It's my agent and my manager," Tad said, sounding annoyed.

"Tad?" his agent Richard called.

"Sir Tad?" his manager added.

"This is a nightmare," Tad complained. "What are you guys doing here?" he called to the door, which he hadn't made a move to open. If he let them into his room, it would be bringing Hollywood here, to Fraziers Bottom.

"Let us in and we'll tell you!" his agent replied.

Tad crossed his arms in front of his stomach. "I'm not going to let them in."

"You can't just leave people out in the hall!" Rosalee said.

"Why not?"

"Because that's not the way you act!" she cried.

"Oh." Tad nodded and moved toward the door as the knocking continued to get louder. He turned around to look at Rosalee one last time before opening it. "I'd like to apologize to both you and myself." Then he pulled open the door, and there they were. The Richard Levys. "Hi, fellas," he said in a bored voice.

"We tried to reach you on your cell phone," his manager Richard said, marching into the room and giving it a disdainful look.

"A fisherman answered," his agent said, following him.

"And you must be Rosalee." His manager stopped in front of her and bowed slightly.

"Yes." Rosalee nodded, and her face turned slightly pink.

"Are you an actress?" Tad's manager asked.

Rosalee shook her head. "No."

"Really? Because you would work."

"Did we come at a bad time?" Tad's agent asked.

"Actually, yes," Tad told them. "What can I do for you guys?"

"Well, Tad." A big grin spread across his agent Richard's face. "Jimmy Ing stopped breathing."

"Huh?" Tad didn't know what he was talking about.

"You got the part!" his manager cried.

"*What!*" Tad screamed. "How?"

His agent grinned. "Seems he saw something that reminded him that he had to have you."

"What was that?" Tad asked.

"Well, it was—" his agent began.

"It was the body of your work!" his manager cut in. "Your resume. Your credits. The reality of you, and of who you are."

His agent nodded slowly, pushing a piece of paper back into his pocket. "That's right. He called me up and he said, 'Who am I kidding? Tad Hamilton has to play this part. There's nobody else.'"

"Nobody else," his manager repeated, apparently in a state of bliss.

"That's what I'm talking about!" Tad yelled as he jumped up and down. "That's what I'm talking about!" He pumped his fist in the air. "That's *exactly* what I'm talking about!"

Rosalee watched Tad jump up and down on the bed like a little kid. He was laughing and whooping like she'd never seen him before. She'd never seen him act like this, period. He was so thrilled to have the part—he must have wanted it very, very badly. Which was funny, because he hadn't mentioned it since their first date, back in Los Angeles.

So what did all this mean? For him—for her— for them?

"So, then, you're leaving?" Rosalee asked timidly after a minute, dreading the answer, even though she already knew what it would be.

"Mm-hmm," his agent said, before Tad could

respond. "You've got fittings all day Monday, and rehearsals start Tuesday. You're back on the beam, pally."

Tad laughed and high-fived both Richards, yelling with excitement.

Rosalee couldn't believe what was happening. "Boy, things happen fast, huh?" she asked. "I mean, you sure can move quickly from movie star to ashram-member-slash-cow-milker and then back to movie star again." She didn't mean to sound so critical, but it came out that way.

Tad looked at her, and his smile faded. "You're right."

Rosalee could see that she'd just ruined his moment. She didn't mean to do that—she was just a little bit hurt, that's all. "No, it's cool," she said. "You are who you are. And you're great."

Tad looked at her for another minute. Then he said, "I'm going to turn it down."

"What?" Rosalee asked, stunned. Was he really?

"*What?*" his agent nearly screamed.

"*Hooah?*" his manager stuttered.

"You're a hundred percent right," Tad said to Rosalee. "I came here vowing to change my priorities. And now, at the first opportunity, I'm abandoning that."

As happy as Rosalee was to know that he believed in her, she didn't want him to be unhappy because of his recent change of heart. "Tad, come on," she said. "You're not turning down the part.

We both know that. You nearly high-fived these poor men into the hospital!"

Tad paced around the room, as much as he could in such a small space with three other people in it. The expression on his face went from happiness to confusion to happiness to agony. Finally he said, "Fellas, you want to give us a minute?"

"Of course," his agent said.

"We will be *right* behind that door." His manager pointed to the hotel room door.

"We will be in the *lobby*." They both shuffled out the door, Tad giving them a little help. He closed the door behind them and threw the dead bolt. Then he turned to Rosalee, who was perched on the side of the bed. "I want you to go with me," Tad said, sitting down beside her.

"What?"

"I'm not taking that part unless you go with me," Tad told her. "I'm never taking anything or going anywhere again, unless you take it and go there with me."

"Really?" Rosalee squeaked.

"Have you been listening? I love you, Rosalee."

She gazed into Tad's eyes. She believed him—she did. And yet…he was Tad Hamilton. He had a reputation. "How many times in your life have you said that?" she asked him.

Tad bit his lip. "Not counting the movies?"

"Not counting."

Tad thought it over for a minute before answering.

"Hmm. Well, I've said it a few times," he confessed. "But I never knew what it meant."

That wasn't exactly what Rosalee wanted to hear. If he'd thought he was in love before, and that hadn't been true, then how much could she count on that now? "I guess you'll have to turn down the part, then," she told him. "Because I can't go with you, Tad. You don't love me. You want to love me. And maybe someday you might've loved me. But what you love right now is the idea of me. And that's not enough," Rosalee concluded. She could hardly believe she was turning down the chance to leave with Tad Hamilton, but she had to stay true to what she believed. Tad was looking at her with sad, puppy-dog eyes, as if she were breaking his heart.

"You can't love someone for what they stand for, or what they seem to be," she continued. "You've got to love them for their details, for the things that are true of them and only them."

"I do love you for your details, Rosalee."

"You don't. You couldn't possibly. You don't even know them."

Tad scooted closer to her, put his hand on her leg, and looked directly into her eyes. "You have six smiles," he said.

At first Rosalee thought that he was joking.

"What?"

"You have six smiles, Rosie. One when something really makes you laugh," Tad said. "One when you're just laughing out of politeness. One when you make plans. One when you make fun of yourself." He rubbed small circles on her thigh as he talked. "One when you're uncomfortable. And one when you're talking about your friends."

Rosalee couldn't move. She could hardly remember to breathe. No one had ever said anything that romantic to her before. No one had even come close. "Wow," she exhaled.

"I told you," Tad said.

Rosalee looked at him with newfound admiration. "You *do* love me."

Tad laughed. "I *know!*"

"That's so much better than any speech from any of your movies," she said. *So much better,* she thought.

Tad looked a little embarrassed to have made such an impassioned plea. "So…you'll go?" he asked.

Will I go? I'd be crazy not to! She wanted to scream at the top of her lungs, to jump up and down on the bed the way Tad did. Instead she nodded, smiling, and calmly told him, "Yes."

"I knew you would! You know why?" Tad asked excitedly.

"Why?" Rosalee grinned.

"Because that was smile number six you had, there—the one where you make plans."

Rosalee threw her arms around him and hugged him tightly. They kissed as if there were no tomorrow, as if they hadn't just decided to take this major, life-changing trip together.

"What are you thinking?" Tad whispered in her ear.

"Nothing," Rosalee said. "I'm done thinking. If somehow I'm making a mistake, I no longer want to know."

"You're not making a mistake," Tad assured her, and right now, Rosalee believed him, one hundred percent. Everything felt so right.

"When do we leave?" she asked.

Tad grinned at her and leaped off the bed. "How soon can you be ready?"

CHAPTER **THIRTEEN**

Pete stopped at a traffic light a block from Li'l Dickens. He glanced up at the brightly lit billboard at the side of the road. It had a picture of Tad Hamilton on it, and he was crushing a pack of cigarettes in his hand. TAD HAMILTON SAYS STOP SMOKING, said the headline.

Pete sighed in disgust. He should climb up the billboard and spray-paint "Start" over "Stop."

He was so sick of all the phoniness associated with Tad Hamilton that he could scream. Instead, he headed into Li'l Dickens, sat at the bar, and ordered a whiskey on the rocks.

He didn't drink whiskey, he quickly realized as he sipped from his glass. Who was he trying to kid? But he felt like he needed something strong.

Angelica propped her elbows on the bar and gazed at him. "You know, as a bartender you do learn to kind of recognize those customers who… need to talk."

"Oh, I'm fine, Angelica." Pete tried to take another sip of the whiskey, but he couldn't do it without making a face. It tasted like cough syrup. Strong cough syrup.

"Uh, no, Pete." Angelica shook her head. "You… you really need to talk."

Pete looked at her, trying to figure out if she was making a move on him again, or just trying to be a friend. He decided "friend," partly because she was not trying to show any cleavage at the moment, and partly because he really did need someone to talk to. "Man, I really do," he agreed.

"So talk," Angelica prompted him. "I'm just gonna wipe a glass, if that isn't too much of a cliché."

"No, go ahead." Pete ran his finger around the top of his glass. "So, um, I think Rosalee might be, uh, falling in love with Tad Hamilton."

"Yeah—you didn't have to be a bartender to see that one coming," Angelica said as she placed a glass on the shelf.

"The problem is that I, uh…I'm in love with Rosalee," Pete admitted. He hadn't said it out loud before, and it felt sort of strange.

Angelica stopped drying glasses to look at him for a second. "You know, I always thought maybe you were."

Pete had a feeling it had been more obvious to

everyone else than it had been to him. "Well, you were right."

"How much do you love her?" Angelica asked.

"What?" *Talk about blunt,* Pete thought. "What does that mean?"

"Well, is it 'love,' 'big love,' or 'great love'?" Angelica wanted to know.

Maybe, Pete thought, *he wasn't drinking enough for this particular conversation.* "Define your terms," he said.

"'Love' you get over in two months," Angelica explained. "'Big love' in two years. And 'great love'…"

Pete almost didn't want to know the answer. "Yes?"

"Great love changes your life." Angelica gazed dreamily across the bar.

Pete shifted uncomfortably on the bar stool. "I was afraid you were going to say something like that."

Angelica's eyes went wide. "Oh God, it's great love!"

Pete sighed. "Yeah. Isn't that…great?"

"Well, you gotta win her back," Angelica said matter-of-factly—as if it were no big deal, as if it were something Pete could really do.

"Trust me, Angelica," he said. "I've tried everything."

Angelica set down her last glass and looked at

him. "What did she say when you told her you love her?"

When I told her I love her? Uh, when was that exactly? He'd been meaning to get around to that. "Okay, I haven't done that, actually," he told Angelica, "but I've done everything else."

"Well, what did she say when you kissed her?" Angelica asked.

Pete drummed his fingers against the bar. "Okay, those would be the only two things I haven't done."

Angelica threw up her hands. "Well, what have you done?"

"I have...*very unsubtly* implied how I feel," Pete said proudly, sitting up a little straighter now.

Angelica shook her head, looking disgusted with him. "Okay, get up."

"What?"

"Get off the bar stool," Angelica commanded.

"Angelica—" Pete tried to protest, but she wouldn't let him.

"Great love is a rare and extraordinary gift, Pete. If you feel it and you don't do everything in your power to reach for it, then you're basically just slapping life in the face."

Pete laughed. "Angelica, I hate to tell you. I really don't have much of a chance here."

"As my father told me when I said I'd never get that job at the bar, 'Honey, your odds go up if you file an application.'" She gave Pete a meaningful look.

Pete wasn't budging yet. "I am up against *Tad Hamilton,*" he reminded her.

"You *are* Tad Hamilton," Angelica said.

"What?"

"Don't you see? Everybody's Tad Hamilton to somebody, Pete. Rosalee's Tad Hamilton to you. And you're Tad Hamilton to me."

It took Pete a couple of seconds to realize what a huge compliment Angelica was giving him. "Thank you."

"So start acting like it!" Angelica cried. Then she smiled at him.

Pete looked at her, feeling eternally grateful, if a little uncomfortable. She was right—he had to take action the way Tad Hamilton would. "Okay. You are an excellent bartender," he told Angelica as he stood up to leave.

Pete stood in the doorway for a second, watching Rosalee search through her closet.

"Hi," Pete said softly, trying not to startle her.

Rosalee turned toward him, a surprised expression on her face. "Hi," she said. "How'd you get in?"

What was she talking about? Mr. Futch had been sitting outside on the porch. "How did I get in? I iced the guards and blew the dead bolt," Pete joked.

Rosalee laughed. Pete watched her for a second as she neatened a stack of folded jeans on her bed. This was hard, but he wasn't going to lose his nerve. Angelica's words were still fresh in his mind. *Great love is a rare and extraordinary gift, Pete. If you feel it and you don't do everything in your power to reach for it, then you're basically just slapping life in the face.*

He stepped into the room. "I have something I want to say to you."

"Me, too," Rosalee said, sounding excited. "To you."

"Really?" Pete asked.

She nodded.

"Okay, you go first," Pete told her.

Rosalee shook her head. "No, you."

"No, please, after you." Pete had no idea what she would say, but maybe it had something to do with him. Maybe that was why she looked so happy to see him. She could tell him how she felt, and then he'd tell her, and then...who knew? *Great love,* Pete thought. *This is what it feels like. Here it comes.*

"Okay." Rosalee's big blue eyes were shining as she looked at him. "Tad got the part of a lifetime in a *huge* movie!" she said. "And he asked me to go with him to California for the shoot! We're leaving in the morning. Isn't that great?"

Pete felt like a balloon that had just been popped

with a pin. A very, very sharp pin, actually. "You know," he said, "next time, if you could give me just one more 'No, please after you.'"

Rosalee looked at him expectantly. "What were you going to say?"

Pete felt completely hopeless now. She was leaving town. What point would there be in telling her now? Especially when she was so in love with Tad.

"Oh, um, nothing, it was nothing," he said. "Just, um, travel safely. Enjoy the shoot." Pete turned to leave but then thought better of it. He would tell her. He had to at least try.

Pete turned back around and faced Rosalee, who'd now pulled a suitcase out and was starting to pack it. "And, uh, oh—I remember what it was." He stepped toward Rosalee and put his hand on her waist and kissed her like he'd never kissed anyone before. He could feel her kissing him back, too—she was just as into it as he was!

When their lips separated, Pete looked her in the eye and bravely said, "I love you, Rosalee. And I always have."

She gazed back at him with a glassy look in her eyes. She didn't seem surprised—or upset—or anything, yet.

"And if I've been acting like an idiot...or if I've been a little negative or sarcastic or anything about Tad... I'm not saying I have, but if I have...it's because I've been fighting for you," Pete told her.

This was It. He was laying all his cards on the table. "It's because I don't want to lose you to Tad Hamilton—or to anyone else. It's because you're the one."

CHAPTER **FOURTEEN**

Rosalee just stared at Pete. She'd never seen him like this. She'd never heard him *talk* like this—so seriously, so emotionally. And they'd definitely never kissed before—she felt like she was going to keel over from the shock of it all.

Pete was looking at her intently, waiting for her to speak. And she didn't know what to tell him. Her emotions were whirling around inside of her.

"So, um, any reaction to any of this at all?" Pete asked anxiously. "Because now would be an excellent time."

Suddenly Rosalee knew exactly how she felt.

"Now? You kiss me *now*?" She shoved Pete's chest with her hands.

He just looked at her with those hazel, pleading, talk-to-me eyes of his, and she almost wanted to kick him. How dare he come here tonight and pour out his heart to her? His timing was terrible.

"You say this to me *now,* after seventeen years of being my friend?" she demanded. "The night before I'm supposed to go to California with another guy?"

"Um…yes to all questions," Pete said with a shrug.

"I can't think about this now!" Rosalee told him. "I have to pack."

"You can't answer the most important question I'll ever ask in my life, because you have to *pack?*" Pete asked.

"Not just pack. I have a load of whites in the dryer." Rosalee folded a sweater and placed it carefully into the suitcase. "My dad called our relatives in San Clemente—they're expecting me. Things are in the works." She kept moving, afraid that if she stopped she wouldn't know what to do or say.

"What's in your heart, Rosalee?" Pete pressed. "What's in your heart?"

My heart is a jumble, a tangled web, a—I don't know what it is! Rosalee thought, confusion taking over her. "I…I…I cannot, I can't, and I won't and I will not and should not and ought not and do not!" she stuttered.

"Huh?" Pete was staring at her.

"Am I making myself clear?" Rosalee demanded.

"No," Pete said.

"Well, I stand by my statement." Rosalee continued to fold clothes. She couldn't explain herself, nor could she look at Pete anymore.

"Just say you feel nothing for me. Just say it." Pete stood beside her for a second, waiting for an answer.

What was she supposed to do, tell him that she loved him, too? But she loved Tad. Well, she did love Pete, as a friend, of course. But it wasn't the same as the way she felt about Tad, was it? She was utterly, entirely confused.

"You can't, can you?" Pete asked.

No, Rosalee thought. *But I also can't change my mind about Tad on the spot, either.* "I'm sorry this is the way we had to say good-bye," she said without looking at him.

"I'm sorry, too," Pete said. He turned to go, and Rosalee looked up then and sadly watched him walk out the door. She had no idea if leaving Pete behind was the right thing to do, but it was what she was doing. She couldn't back out now.

"You okay, Pete?" Mr. Futch asked, looking up from his book as Pete walked out of the house onto the front porch.

"Yes, sir," Pete said glumly. Only if "okay" meant "wretched."

Mr. Futch closed his book and set it on the porch railing. "Listen, Pete. Obviously we've all been a little seduced by Tad Hamilton's presence." Mr. Futch removed the baseball cap he was wearing, which had a "Project Greenlight" logo on its front.

"No one more so than me. But that doesn't mean I don't know, at the end of the day, who cares about my daughter the most, and who she would be with if the world were fair."

Wow, Pete thought. This was going above and beyond for Mr. Futch. "Well, it's not, so..."

"No, it's not," Mr. Futch agreed. "You know, when I was your age, I was completely in love with Eleanor Hershey. Of the chocolate Hersheys. The Hershey chocolates." Mr. Futch waved his hand in the air. "You know what I mean. She was a great girl. Completely unpretentious. I actually met her filling her Cadillac up with gas. Anyway, there was this French guy. He was really rich. He owned, like...France. I didn't stand a chance."

Was this supposed to be a pep talk, Pete wondered. Because if so, it wasn't really helping, considering Mr. Futch obviously had not married this Eleanor person.

"It happens that way sometimes, Pete," Mr. Futch went on. "It shouldn't, but it does. Sometimes Goliath kicks the crap out of David. Nobody bothers to tell that story."

Pete just looked at him and let the futility of his entire life sink in. "Thanks, Mr. Futch. I feel much better."

Rosalee walked slowly beside Cathy toward the private jet waiting for them. In front of her, Tad was busy discussing details with his agent and manager, her dad beside them, listening eagerly. Rosalee had only flown a few times in her life, and except for the last time, she'd always flown coach. Now she was about to board a private G-8 with Tad Hamilton. So much had changed—so quickly.

They came to a stop near the plane, and Cathy and Rosalee's dad both stared openmouthed at the jet. Rosalee was too preoccupied thinking about what she was leaving behind to be impressed. Maybe she was doing the right thing by leaving with Tad. Then again, maybe she wasn't.

"You all right?" Cathy asked.

"No," Rosalee admitted.

"You sure you know what you're doing?"

Rosalee shook her head. "No."

"Ever in your life feel more confused or alone?" Cathy said.

Doubtful, Rosalee thought as she glanced over at Tad. "No."

"Well, have a nice flight!" Cathy teased her as they approached the steps to the plane. Rosalee had never been out here on the actual "tarmac" before. She felt as if she were really in a movie now.

"I hear the G-8 has a range of almost eight thousand miles, and yet it's nimble enough to tuck into some of those real tricky airports, like St. Bart's," her father was saying to Tad. Rosalee had to laugh—he was still trying to impress the movie star.

"That's right, Henry," Tad said.

"Henry, you are one mediocre high-concept comedy away from a meaningful career in show business," Tad's manager told him.

Mr. Futch smiled, looking very pleased. "So, we'll see you after principal photography?" he asked as he hugged Rosalee good-bye.

"Yes, Daddy." Rosalee quickly hugged Cathy, too. She didn't want to drag this good-bye out any longer. It was hard for her, leaving Fraziers Bottom. And it was really strange not to have Pete here.

"You guys don't mind not flying with us, right?" Tad asked the two Richards. "We kind of need the privacy."

"It's fine," his agent said with a shrug.

"Yeah, we're really looking forward to our nasty commercial flight," his manager said.

"We'll be fine," his agent insisted.

"I always wanted to have a layover in Cincinnati." Tad's manager looked disgusted by the concept.

"We will be absolutely fine," Tad's agent repeated.

"And then another one in Chicago…we'll be in L.A. by April," his manager predicted.

"We couldn't be finer." Agent Richard smiled uneasily.

"I didn't get into show business to fly on a commercial flight!" Richard the manager suddenly burst out. "I don't want to catch a cold! I don't want to sit near obese people! I don't want to eat microwaved nuts! I don't want to cringe at the hairstyles on the flight attendants! I don't want to hear the captain butcher the English language as he makes an announcement every four minutes about which way he's turning and how high he's flying! I don't care which way he's turning! And I don't want to see a sign in the bathroom that says, 'May we suggest that you clean up in consideration of the next passenger'! I want to go with you, Tad! I want to go with you!" his manager cried, on the verge of tears.

Tad's agent started to pull him away, back toward the terminal. "We'll be fine," he said yet again.

Tad took Rosalee's hand and helped her up the steps to the plane. Rosalee turned around at the top and exchanged smiles with Cathy. Then she waved good-bye to her friend and her dad, and ducked inside Tad's private jet.

CHAPTER **FIFTEEN**

Tad paced back and forth in the plane's cabin, talking on the telephone with Jimmy Ing about the upcoming project. As good as it had felt to get away for a while—it felt even better to be back.

"Well, Jimmy, I think it's really important that my character have a past," Tad said after listening to Jimmy's vision for the movie. "You know, before the film. And a future, you know, after it."

He glanced over at Rosalee and smiled and waved to her. She was perched on the zebra-print sofa, looking almost too pretty in a cute blue dress. She was leafing through a fashion magazine, waiting patiently for this call to be over.

"Well, I figure he never got enough love as a child, you know?" Tad said, trying to give his character some weight. "He got almost enough love, but not quite enough. Or maybe he got enough love, but he didn't realize it was enough. Or maybe…"

He noticed Rosalee putting down the magazine as if she were suddenly very bored by it.

"I was thinking that he should be very well dressed, always, Jimmy," Tad continued. "Versace, Charvet…There are these shoes I saw in New York that I think are exactly what this character is about."

Rosalee let out a loud sigh and sort of slumped on the sofa. *Uh-oh,* Tad thought. *She doesn't look happy. She doesn't seem even half as happy as I feel right now.*

"Jimmy…listen, we're hitting a little turbulence. Can I call you back in a few minutes? Thank you, sir." Tad hung up the cabin phone and went over to Rosalee, sitting across from her in a red leather chair. "You okay?" he asked.

"Mm-hmm," Rosalee said.

That wasn't very convincing. "You sure?" Tad pressed.

"Mm-hmm. I mean, I'm a little nervous, for some reason. There's a little nervous something inside my, um, self," she said. "But that's only natural, right? I mean, this is a pretty huge thing for me to be doing. Kind of a great leap of faith. But I have that faith. In you. So I'm fine." She sat up a little straighter and smoothed her dress on her lap. "This is going to be great. Can't you tell by my smile?"

"Um, uh-huh." *No, not really,* Tad thought.

"Which smile is it?" Rosalee asked.

Which smile? "Huh?" he asked.

"Which number smile?"

"Oh." Now Tad remembered. Only he didn't quite remember exactly how it went. But that was okay, right? There was no way she'd remember something he said in the excitement of the moment, down to the last detail. "Um, smile number six," he said boldly. If you said things with confidence, he'd learned, people tended to believe you, whether you were right or not.

But Rosalee didn't look as if she was buying it—yet. "Six? Wasn't six when I'm talking about my friends?"

Truthfully, he had no idea. He hated lying to Rosalee, but he didn't have a choice. "Oh, right, right, right. It's number two," Tad said.

Rosalee's eyebrows narrowed. "I thought smile number two was when something really made me laugh."

Tad leaned toward her and looked into her eyes. He had to turn the charm meter up another notch if he was going to get out of this one. "Two and a half, then," he said with a grin.

She nodded and smiled at him, but Tad couldn't help noticing that her smile looked fake—like the night at the Ivy when she was attempting to paste one on for the media and hold it for ten minutes, and she failed.

Tad looked at her for another minute, at her

innocence and her vulnerability. She had been so good to him. She had given him a new lease on life—in so many ways. She'd showed him there were more important things in life than being popular, and rich, and handsome. She'd helped him find the person he used to be before this layer of fakeness built up on him.

So how could he treat her this way, by lying to her in return? She deserved better than that. He expected more of himself now. It was time to face the truth and admit who he really was. And as much as he hated it, he wasn't the guy who deserved Rosalee.

He looked away from her, breaking her gaze. "Rosalee, I didn't know about your six smiles," he finally admitted. "Pete told me about them. He trapped me in the toilet and told me about your six smiles and various other amazing aspects of you. And then he made me swear I wouldn't break your heart, or he said he'd tear me to pieces, either with his bare hands or his rhetoric." Tad took a deep breath and continued. "I stole the speech to get you to come with me. I lied. I'm sorry. I know you're gonna be very upset." He looked up at her, half-expecting to see her in tears, and half-expecting to see her pick up a martini shaker to hit him over the head with it.

But she did neither. She just said, "Pete told you about the six smiles?" She seemed very intense and very business like, as if this were a courtroom drama and she was starring in the lawyer role.

Tad nodded. "That's right."

"He trapped you in the toilet?" Rosalee demanded.

"Yes…"

"And he made you swear you wouldn't break my heart?" she asked.

"Uh-huh." It was all just like he'd told her the first time. Why did she need to go over it again?

"Or he said he'd tear you to pieces?" Rosalee said.

"Yes." *Your honor,* he felt like adding.

"With either his bare hands or his rhetoric?" Rosalee said.

"You've got it."

"That is just…" Rosalee frowned.

Tad cringed a little, waiting for her to explode, to yell, to throw something at him. That was how his usual fights with girlfriends went.

But then Rosalee smiled—not just any smile, but smile number 200, probably. Bigger and brighter than any smile he'd ever seen. And her eyes were filled with tears—real tears. "*So* adorable!" she finished the sentence.

"Huh?" Tad was stunned.

"Pete loves me!" Rosalee said excitedly.

"Yes, he does."

"No, I know, but I mean he *really* loves me!" she cried.

"Okay…" Tad said slowly.

"More than anyone else has ever loved me."

"Well—" Tad was about to interject that he really did love her.

"Or ever will love me," Rosalee declared.

"Um..." *That could be true,* Tad thought.

"And I..." She stopped for a second, as if she were weighing all the options in her mind. "Do you think it's possible to love someone all your life and not realize it until something happens to make you see?"

Tad stared at her, trying to place the speech. "What's that from?" he asked.

"It's not from anything—I'm just saying it to you."

"Oh." *Oops.* He smiled, feeling a little embarrassed. Wait a second. Was he getting dumped? Tad Hamilton didn't get dumped.

"I'm sorry," Rosalee said.

"No, no, it's okay," Tad said, acting more chipper about everything than he felt. He was losing a really great, really incredible girl. To a Piggly Wiggly guy. "I'm all right, I'm okay. I'm all right. I'm okay," he repeated. "Pete...Pete deserves you," he told Rosalee.

"Thank you." She nodded and put her hands on his for a second.

Then Tad sat back in his chair. "Man, what a week. Fell in love for the first time. Got my heart broken for the first time. Was honorable for the first time. Got bitten in the butt for being honorable for the first time. Bought a farm. It's a lot to absorb."

"I'm sorry about the broken heart part," Rosalee offered.

"No, no, it feels good, actually. I mean, it feels bad—very bad, actually." He coughed. "Really just sensationally bad—but also good. It feels like the beginning of something," Tad told her.

Rosalee laughed. "Well, good."

"Thank you for showing me who I can be," Tad told her honestly. "I knew it was a good idea to come here."

Rosalee smiled at him, and he looked into her eyes. He knew this was a good-bye that was going to stick with him. She wasn't like the others. "I hope I'll still see you sometimes," he said.

"You'll see me if you want to," she said with a cute little shrug. "And anyway, I'll sure see *you*."

Tad thought about their night at the Rialto. He was glad he'd be able to picture Rosalee going to his movies in the future, and he'd know exactly what the place looked like, and what row she liked to sit in, and that she liked Milk Duds and not Raisinettes. Of course, she'd be at the movies with Pete, probably. Just like she always used to be, only things would be different between them.

"I think I should take you home now," Tad told her with a charming smile. Then he walked over to pick up the cabin phone to call the cockpit and tell the pilot to turn back. He was glad he had something to do, because it gave him a moment to collect himself.

Tad couldn't believe the changes the last week had brought to his life. He'd fallen in love, really in love. He'd had his heart broken. He was feeling very torn up inside. It felt awful, it felt terrible, it felt...*real*, Tad realized, like nothing he'd ever felt before. Before Rosalee, he wasn't even sure he had had a heart to break. Maybe he had lost the girl this time, but he felt like he'd gotten something valuable in return.

CHAPTER SIXTEEN

Rosalee jumped out of her car and ran to Pete's apartment building. She had to get to him right away. She wouldn't feel okay until she saw Pete, until she told him how she felt.

When she got to his door, she knocked on it as hard as she could. "Pete? Pete? *Pete!*" Rosalee called urgently. How could he not be answering her? "Pete! Pe—"

The door swung open. Angelica was standing there, of all people. Rosalee was almost too stunned to talk, but she managed to utter, "Not Pete."

Angelica looked at her, wide-eyed, as if she were equally surprised.

"Wow. I'm too late. Well. Wow," Rosalee stammered. "Good for you, Angelica. You got your guy. Whereas I just...blew it." She felt her heart sinking as she tried to make sense of it all. "Sorry to...disturb. I hope you'll be...very happy together." Rosalee turned away from the doorway.

"Are you finished?" Angelica asked.

Rosalee stopped and turned to face her. "Huh?"

"I'm just here because Pete asked me to box up some stuff," Angelica said.

"Oh." Somehow this seemed like good news. Angelica was only in Pete's apartment to help him pack. But then it struck Rosalee that if he was packing, he must be leaving town. "Why? Where's he going?" she asked.

"Richmond. And he isn't going, he's gone," Angelica said quietly, clearly saddened by the fact.

"Gone? To Richmond?" Rosalee couldn't believe her ears. "He can't go to Richmond. Why'd he go to Richmond?" She'd flown back to find him, and he was on his way to Richmond? What kind of sense did that make?

"Because that's the way it is with great love," Angelica said.

"What do you mean?"

Angelica sighed. "I cannot believe that I am taking my work home with me." She waited a beat, then explained, "When great love is rejected, Rosalee, something inside a man dies. It's like...life broke its promise to him. And there isn't ever any mending that. Not down deep."

Rosalee felt a pang on Pete's behalf. Why did

she have to reject him, why did she have to hurt him like that?

"So all he can do is run away as fast and far as he can...to someplace like Richmond, Virginia," Angelica continued. "Where he can meet the girl he'll love second-most, and try to forget what happened across the state line."

Rosalee just stood in the doorway, feeling hopeless. She'd turned down Pete and he was lost to her forever.

"Unless..." Angelica went on.

"Unless what?" Rosalee asked eagerly.

"Unless you get to him before he closes the book on you."

Rosalee's eyes lit up. "How long before he closes the book?"

"Hard to say. But once it's closed, it's closed," Angelica said. "Finished. Gone. Dead. Crushed. Beaten. Buried. Lost for all time in a sea of—"

"Angelica?" Rosalee interrupted.

"Yes?"

"I get it," Rosalee said. She had to find Pete as soon as possible.

"Okay."

Rosalee smiled at Angelica. She knew how much Angelica loved Pete, and how hard this must be for her to tell Rosalee how and where to find him—to tell her what she needed to do to earn Pete's love. "Thank you!" she said warmly.

Angelica nodded, and Rosalee ran out the door, back to her car. She had to get to Route 64 and catch him before he got to Richmond. She floored the gas on the highway entrance ramp and quickly built speed.

The only hope she had was that Pete's old Mustang didn't go all that fast, no matter how hard you pushed the accelerator. She cruised down the highway, blasting music as she drove faster and faster. When she saw Pete, she was going to throw her arms around him, and she wasn't going to let him go.

That is, if he'd let her.

Pete headed east to the tune of "By the Time I Get to Phoenix" by Glen Campbell, which didn't make any sense at all. He would never get to Phoenix. He didn't want to get to Phoenix. At least it wasn't a bad night for traveling—there was a nearly full moon that lit up the road ahead of him.

His dog, Rochelle, sat beside him in the passenger seat looking droopy and sad, just like Pete. Yes, it was true that not many people decided to make major life changes in the middle of the night. But then, most people hadn't been rejected by Rosalee.

Glen Campbell wasn't making him feel any better. Pete changed the radio station and sat back, focusing on the road. The strains of another miserably depressing song, "Seasons in the Sun," could be heard over the roar of his engine at highway speed. He tried again. Now he was listening to "Don't They Know It's the End of the World." He switched to AM, hoping to find something better, maybe a decent call-in show.

"Yeah, so, anyway, I lost all my money, and my house and my car," a man was saying. "And my friends...and my stamp collection, and my silhouettes of the presidents, and my family won't speak to me anymore. But hey, at least I got a girlfriend. I mean, I'm not a *total* loser."

Pete frowned, flipped back to FM, and kept searching. Finally the radio landed on a decent song—"I Wished on the Moon" by Billie Holiday.

He'd barely accomplished this when a car pulled up beside him and honked its horn loudly and insistently. "What's your prob—" Pete began.

But then he saw that it was Rosalee. Rosalee! What was she doing here? He did a double-take to make sure he wasn't seeing things. Yes, it was definitely her. Pete was so surprised to see her that he swerved to the left, and then to the right. He went off the right side of the road, narrowly missing a fencepost, slamming into a mailbox and knocking it over before the car screeched to a halt.

Rosalee pulled up behind him, and Pete cautiously stepped out of the Mustang, leaving the door open, the Billie Holiday song wafting into the night air.

"You okay?" Rosalee called to Pete as soon as she got out of the car.

"Absolutely." Pete ran a hand through his spiky brown hair. "I meant to do that."

They walked toward each other, their feet crunching on the gravel. Rosalee opened her mouth to say something, but then closed it. Pete's eyes widened as he waited for her to talk. She was the one who'd tracked him down—she was the one who had to speak first.

Rosalee tried again, opening her mouth as though she was about to say something. But then she closed it again. Pete just looked at her, trying to be patient as he desperately waited for her to say something—anything—about what she was doing here. This was a big moment, a huge moment. They both knew it.

Finally Rosalee smiled, and said, "You've got five smiles, Pete. One when you think someone's an idiot. One when you think someone's *really* an idiot. One when you get all dressed up. One when you're singing Barry White. And one...when you're looking at me."

Pete gazed at her for a minute, amazed by this speech, impressed she knew so much about him, and completely captivated by how beautiful she looked right now. The Billie Holiday song was still playing on his car radio, and Pete suddenly realized where he'd heard it before. That Tad Hamilton movie, the one where Tad played the Army lieutenant—this same song had been used in the movie during a scene very much like this one.

Pete looked at Rosalee. He couldn't believe that real life was working out like a Tad Hamilton movie. Pete knew this would probably be the one of the corniest things he ever did in his life, but Rosalee was worth it. "I can't believe I'm about to do this, but..." He held out his hand toward her.

Rosalee's face slowly blossomed into a beautiful smile. They raced toward one another and she leapt into Pete's arms, kissing him fiercely and passionately, kissing Pete like no one had ever kissed him before.

Wow, Pete thought as he and Rosalee began to dance to "I Wished on the Moon," with the moon shining down on them on this beautiful, clear night. It really was just like a movie.

EPILOGUE

Rosalee stared at the screen. Was it her, or was the actress in the movie wearing her hair exactly the way that Rosalee did?

She was with Pete and Cathy at the Rialto, watching the newest Tad Hamilton movie. But this wasn't just any Tad Hamilton movie—this was *the* movie, the one directed by Jimmy Ing, the one she'd almost left Fraziers Bottom for so that she could be by Tad's side while he filmed it.

She glanced over at Pete in the darkened theater. A year later, she was still incredibly, amazingly glad she'd come back to town, that she'd decided to turn around and come home to Pete.

Up on the screen, Tad was sitting on a park bench next to the latest hot, young, beautiful actress in Hollywood. He was dressed exactly the way he'd been describing for his character that day on his jet. *Everything worked out for Tad the way he wanted it to*, Rosalee thought, *and I'm really happy for him*.

"May I kiss you good-bye?" Tad asked his co-star now.

"Oh, I think you might maybe may," she replied.

Tad leaned in to kiss her, but she held up her hand to stop him. Then she reached into her mouth and pulled out a small retainer. They smiled at each other, and then Tad tilted his co-star's mouth toward his, and their lips met in a passionate, no-holds-barred kiss.

Rosalee laughed and applauded loudly, cheering for Tad along with everyone beside her—including Pete.

"I have *got* to get a retainer," Cathy announced.